# 23 Under 1 Roof

## Making Dreams Come true

Ruth Rappaport

**23 Under 1 Roof** /
Making Dreams Come True

Copyright © 2023 by Tfutza Publications
ISBN: 979-8-88673-048-7

P.O.B. 50036
Beitar Illit 90500
Tel: (02) 650-9400
tfutza1@gmail.com

First published in Hebrew as:
*Esrim V'echad B'bayit Echad: Magshimim Chalomot*

Written by Ruth Rappaport
Cover illustration and design by Yoni Gerstein
Inside illustrations by Ruth Beifus
Translated by R. Cywiak
Edited by Sara Miriam Gross
Copyedited by Cindy Scarr
Proofread by M. Deutscher
Typeset by Deena Weinberg

Distributed by:
**Israel Bookshop Publications**
501 Prospect Street
Lakewood, NJ 08701
Tel: (732) 901-3009
Fax: (732) 901-4012
www.israelbookshoppublications.com
info@israelbookshoppublications.com

**Printed in Israel**

| Distributed in Israel by: | Distributed in Europe by: | Distributed in Australia by: | Distributed in S. Africa |
|---|---|---|---|
| **Tfutza Publications** | **Lehmanns** | **Gold's Book & Gift Company** | **Kollel Bookshop** |
| P.O.B. 50036 | Unit E Viking Industrial Park | 3- 13 William Street | Ivy Common |
| Beitar Illit 90500 | Rolling Mill Road, | Balaclava 3183 | 107 William Rd, Norwo |
| Tel: (02) 650-9400 | Jarrow , Tyne & Wear NE32 3DP | 613-9527-8775 | Johannesburg 2192 |
| tfutza1@gmail.com | 44-191-430-0333 | | 27-11-728-1822 |

# Contents

# The Schneider Children

**Chevy,** 21 — the oldest of the family and assistant mother, now married

**Binyamin (Benny),** 19 — mature and serious, a diligent learner

**Ayala,** 18 — Benny's almost-twin, who worries about everyone else

**Nechamy,** 17 — goodhearted and friendly, one of the children's favorites

**Avigdor,** 16 — easygoing and smiley, with a calm personality

**Chani,** 14½ — philosophical and emotional, serious and deep

**Motty,** 13½ — leader of the "Schneider middlies," active, talented and lively

**Miri,** 13½ — Motty's twin, mature and friendly, talented and well-liked by all

**Etty,** 12½ — lively and smart, feels lonely stuck between two sets of twins

**Riki,** 11½ — energetic and exuberant, serves as the spokesperson for the children in all kinds of situations

**Shevi,** 11½ — Riki's twin, dreamy and scatterbrained, tends to get into trouble

**Yoni,** 10½ — brilliant in learning, a masmid, investigates everything

**Lali,** 9 — loves animals and adventures of all kinds

**Sruly,** 8 — helps Lali in everything she does

**Shuey,** 7 — very mature for his age, loves adult company and tries to follow his father wherever he can

**Bentzy,** 6 — the oldest of the youngest set of children, feels like their leader

**Tully,** 5 — a bit mischievous with unbelievable and unpredictable ideas

**Gila,** 3 — likes to feel big

**Tammy,** 2 — Eli's twin

**Eli,** 2 — Tammy's twin

**Tzivi,** almost a year old — a calm, delightful baby

## Chapter 1

### *Aunt Chana's Surprise*

"I have a surprise for you!" Aunt Chana announced as she entered the room with a secretive look on her face. Miri, Lali, and Shevi looked up curiously. They were busy preparing Welcome Home signs for Abba and Ima, who were supposed to come home the day after tomorrow.

"You aren't asking what it is," she chuckled. "Polite girls, aren't you? Well, then, I'll tell you: There's a wonderful fair that's going to be held here, along the promenade. They got permission from the city, and all the proceeds go to a *chessed* organization. There'll be performances, raffles, rides…do you want to go?"

"Of course!!" Lali jumped up happily. Miri glared at her, and then said politely, "But won't it be too hard for you, Aunt Chana?"

"Why would it be hard?" she asked.

"To take us there, get organized, bring us back…."

"That's hard?!" She seemed almost offended. "I'd be happy to take you! After all, I'm the one who suggested it!"

"We'll have to ask Ima," Miri said in the same serious tone. "And see if she agrees."

"Of course," Aunt Chana agreed. "I'll call and ask."

She left the room, and the girls began to discuss the plans.

"A fair? Here? Why here in Yaffo?" Miri narrowed her eyes suspiciously. "Is it a *frum chessed* organization?" Shevi wondered aloud. "Because this area really isn't *frum.*"

"Why are you asking so many questions?" Lali could not understand her sisters. "You're being offered something fun — enjoy it!"

"We have to find out if it's okay."

"If Aunt Chana is suggesting it, and Ima knows Aunt Chana and trusts her, so it's for sure okay!"

Aunt Chana returned to the room. "Your mother agrees," she said with a half-smile. "But she told me not to take the little boys along. That will be their punishment for the little voyage they decided to take without asking anyone...."

The girls exchanged uneasy glances.

"What is it?" Aunt Chana asked. She noticed that something was bothering the girls.

"Perhaps," Miri whispered, "but really, only if it's okay with you...could we bring our other sisters, too? From the start they were disappointed that they couldn't be here with us."

"Of course you can. I was thinking of taking them!" exclaimed Aunt Chana. "We already spoke about it, your mother and I, and Ayala as well. We've got it all figured out. Your sisters will come and enjoy the fair together with you."

"How nice!" Shevi squealed. Then she blushed like a rose. "I...I just really didn't want Riki to miss it," she stammered with embarrassment.

Aunt Chana smiled at her fondly. "You're a wonderful girl, and I'm sure your sister is so happy to be your sister."

"Well, they're not just regular sisters," Lali explained earnestly. "They're identical twins."

"So, are we all interested?"

"For sure!" Shevi and Lali cried. Miri, as the oldest among them, had to suppress her excitement and look mature, so she just nodded.

Aunt Chana smiled and left them alone.

"You see, Ima lets," Lali told her sister. "You're just looking for problems."

"I had to make sure she really did let," Miri said defensively. "What do you want? That we should tell her that we're coming and then back out? She'd be so offended."

"And now she's offended that you weren't that excited about it."

"She was not."

"Was too."

"Enough," Shevi said, trying to restore peace. "Let's continue working on the signs. If we're going to the fair tomorrow, we won't have time to finish them afterward."

The girls sat down and got busy with the signs again. In her vivid imagination, Lali pictured the attractive booths along the promenade. She figured that there would be booths filled with flowers and others with balloons, surprises and...animals. And she hoped there would be one booth — even a small one — that would sell animals. Maybe she'd buy a pet with her own money? She could get a baby chick, which would be a friend for Yoni's pigeons, or a big aquarium where she could put her dusky grouper fish. Or maybe she'd buy a little hamster, or a rabbit....

Lali sighed. Ima would never agree, that was for sure. They would not bring any non-kosher animal into the house, Abba had explained firmly.

She had been four at the time, and had looked at Abba with two pools of disappointment in her eyes. "Not even an elephant?" she'd whispered in dismay.

"No," Abba had said with the same seriousness that he gave to everything she said, even the funny things.

"Not even a baby elephant? I saw a cute little elephant in the zoo...exactly the size of my bed."

"If an elephant isn't kosher, it won't come into our house, Lali. That's the rule," Abba said, paying no attention to all the other problems involved in bringing an elephant home: the expensive price, the heavy weight that could make the floor cave in, the huge amounts of food it eats, and the fact that it would quickly grow into a big elephant. Then, of course, they wouldn't be able to control it or keep it in their home....

Lali had been disappointed, but she realized that her parents were absolutely firm about not bringing a non-kosher animal into the house. Since then, she'd thought a lot about it. Okay, then, so why couldn't she bring home a cow? They would have fresh milk each morning, and she'd happily run to milk the cow and drink the milk. Then she'd lead it down the steps, super-carefully (not in the elevator — the cow was too fat) and take her to the grass in their yard. There, she'd eat up the grass and the flowers (Oy, no, not the flowers! Mrs. Berkowitz would be very angry!) Alright, then only the grass, and that would save money on the gardener who wouldn't need to mow the lawn....

"Lali!" Miri called to her.

"What?" She shook herself back to the present, looking at the blue crayon in her hand. "What happened?"

"What are you dreaming about? Why did you stop coloring?"

"I dreamed," Lali sighed deeply, "about a cow grazing in the front yard of our building...."

## Chapter 2

## The Fair

The fair took place the next day.

The middle girls — all six of them — went out with Aunt Chana to the fair. Chani, Miri, Etty, Riki, Shevi, and Lali, the six united Schneiders, as Aunt Chana called them with a chuckle.

"Look, look!" Lali called, sharing her enthusiasm with her sisters. "Look what they did to the promenade!"

Their aunt smiled when she saw their excitement. "Nice, isn't it? This year, the organization decided to make their fair here because of the gorgeous scenery on the promenade."

"They make a fair every year?" Shevi asked shyly.

Aunt Chana nodded. "I help them a bit," she said

modestly, not offering any details about exactly what kind of help she gave. "That's why I know where it is every year. Once it was in Yerushalayim, and another time it was in Haifa. They look for an interesting and attractive location."

From afar they saw flags waving in the breeze, and the roofs of the tents that had been put up. The girls took deep breaths of fresh ocean air, and knew that they were going to have a great time. In each tent there was a different activity. One had a balloon lady who crafted balloons into all kinds of shapes. The second tent had a fire show, and in the third there was a snake exhibit. In the fourth tent, visitors could prepare a small wooden box. And there were many more tents! The girls didn't know which to choose; Aunt Chana gave them each three tickets and let them choose three activities out of fifteen. The girls discussed among themselves what to do, and Aunt Chana went to settle down on a bench to wait for them.

"Let's go to the raffle tent," Lali said excitedly. "Raffles are the most fun! Then we get something to keep!"

"Raffles are fun for the people who win," Miri said coolly. "And we never win."

"We never win???" Etty cried in shock. "Did you forget that we won a car for Yoni?"

"That's because we wanted the car *l'shem Shamayim*," Miri murmured, "not for us but for Yoni."

"So do this raffle *l'shem Shamayim* also — not for yourself but for me." Lali laughed.

Miri was not amused by the joke. "I want to go to the craft tent," she said. "What about you, Chani?"

"I also want to," her older sister agreed. "What about you girls?" She turned to Etty and the twins.

Etty was still hesitating, but Lali had already decided. "I'm going to the snake tent and the raffles," she declared. "I don't mind going myself."

"What do you say, Shevi?" Riki asked her twin.

"Let's go to the raffles also, and to the balloons," Shevi suggested.

"Yes, and to the tent with the pictures!" Riki announced. "We'll take a picture together — that's going to be amazing!"

"Each of us can go wherever she wants," Etty concluded. "Lali, I'm coming with you to the snakes."

The Schneider girls split up, and each pair went to a different tent.

∽∾∽

"It's not fair that we didn't go to the fair," Shuey said as he looked out of the window of his room.

"Of course it's fair," Ayala said to him. "Your behavior was terrible, and even worse than that, very dangerous."

"All I wanted to do was go to England!" Shuey lifted his chin rebelliously. "I missed Ima! And besides, it was all Bentzy's idea!"

"Who, me?" Bentzy leaped out of his place when he heard this accusation.

"Yes, you!" his brother retorted.

"Since when?!"

"Then whose was it?!"

"Yours!"

"Me?! Me?! I suggested an idea, and you got all excited about it, and you upgraded it with your whole list! If we hadn't had that list, we never would have dreamed of going. You brought this long list, so I trusted you that you knew what you were doing."

"Because of my list?!" Shuey howled. "It was your idea!"

"Yes, but you put it into action!" Bentzy hopped on one foot and prepared to spring forward to grab his older brother's peyos.

"Enough, enough," Ayala hushed the two boys, stepping between Bentzy's outstretched hands and Shuey's swinging legs. "Don't fight now! It makes no difference! If one boy has a bad idea, his brother is supposed to convince him that it's a terrible idea, not encourage him."

"You see?!" Bentzy stuck his tongue out at Shuey.

"You see yourself!" Shuey snapped back. "Because the idea was yours!"

"Look," Tully entered the room holding a book, a look of wonder on his face. "It says here that the man took on a false identity. What's a false identity?"

Shuey and Bentzy stopped fighting and listened to their brother.

Ayala was happy for the change of subject. She hurried to answer her little brother: "A false identity is when someone doesn't want people to know who he really is. So he changes things, like his name or his clothing or other things."

"You mean it's like a lie?" Tully tried to understand.

"Yes, exactly. It's an identity that's a lie, because it's not the person's real identity."

"If I say that I'm Bentzy, then my identity is false?" Shuey also tried to understand Ayala's explanation.

"Yes!" Ayala was impressed by how quickly he caught on. "Your real identity is Shuey, and if you tell others that you are Bentzy, you are making up a different identity, a false one."

The children sat for a moment in silence. Ayala was relieved that the fight had stopped, and in her heart, thanked Hashem for Tully and his ideas, and endless questions. She had no way to know that her words had simply set the stage for a new idea....

## Chapter 3

# Dressing Up?

"We simply need a false identity," Shuey said solemnly.

"What?" Bentzy looked at him, puzzled.

"A false identity. If we are not allowed to go there when we're us, then we'll go to the fair under false identities. Yes, yes, a false identity." He enjoyed rolling the new words around on his tongue. "A false identity and that's it. I'm not Shuey and all that, we're someone else. False identities."

"What does that mean?" Tully began to get annoyed. After all, this whole thing about false identities was something he had read about in a book. That made it his idea. So why was Shuey taking all his ideas for himself?

"If Shuey, Bentzy, and Tully are not allowed to go to the

fair, we'll change our identities for different ones!" Shuey explained his idea.

"And then?"

"We'll be able to go! It's not far from here, and I know the way. We walk to the end of the path over there, and then we get there. I know it exactly!"

"I'm not going without permission," Bentzy declared as he wrapped himself in Aunt Chana's entryway rug. "And now, Ayala came here to watch us so we don't do anything silly." He began to dance with the rug wrapped around him; he looked like an Indian doing a war dance.

"Silly things?" Shuey was horrified at the very possibility, as if he was being accused of something unreasonable. "I do silly things?! Never!"

Bentzy ignored him. He continued dancing and hopping, with the rug enveloping him from head to toe.

"I think," Tully said after thinking about it, "that they think that that time we painted our room black, let's say, that that was silly. Or that time we took the boat and sailed ourselves, or—"

"We always had a very important reason!" Shuey was offended.

"Or the time that you went to see the queen." Tully turned to the guilty party — Bentzy.

The rug collapsed from the force of the accusation. "I just wanted to make a special *brachah*!" the wild Indian cried. Tully leaped aside so the rug wouldn't fall on him. "Besides," Bentzy wasn't going to let someone else have the last word, "what about the time that you went to the place where all the suitcases go!"

"Maybe you could be quiet? You're talking so much my ideas are disappearing," Shuey scolded them. "I want to go with a false identity to the fair. If you don't want to, stay home."

"I'm staying here!" Bentzy decided. "You can go wherever you want, I'm staying home!"

Deep down, Shuey hoped that all three would be going, and he couldn't believe his ears. "You're not coming?!"

"No. I'm staying home with Ayala."

"Stay." Shuey pretended he didn't care. "Are you coming, Tully?"

Tully would never refuse an adventure. "Yeah, I'm coming."

"Good," Shuey said. "So now we need only one thing: a false identity. Each one of us will be someone else."

"Can I be Abba, let's say?"

"No!" Shuey cried. He was upset that he hadn't had that idea. "You need to be someone we don't know."

"If we don't know him, how can we be him?" Tully asked.

"Just make it up. Ayala said that a false thing is made up. A false identity is a made-up identity. That someone made up. Let's say that I make up that I'm Mr. Cohen and I live on Chazon Ish Street, and I'm thirty years old."

Tully's eyes sparkled. "How many children do you have?"

"Ummm…I don't know. Not so many. Maybe ten."

"Fine. So who knows that you are now Mr. Cohen and not Shuey Schneider? Cause you look exactly like Shuey looked a minute ago."

"That's no problem," Shuey scoffed. "I'll just dress up!"

"Dress up?!" His two brothers were shocked, and looked at him with admiration. "As Achashverosh? Haman? Mordechai HaYehudi?"

"No!" Shuey cried. "You didn't listen to me! I'm dressing up as Mr. Cohen!"

"Mr. Cohen?" Tully asked. "How are you going to dress up like him?"

"What's the problem?" Shuey answered importantly, as if he dressed up twice a day. "I'll put on a beard from Purim, and a mustache! I'll put sunglasses on top of that and no one will recognize me!"

"And how are you so short?" Bentzy insisted. "There is no one who is thirty who is your height."

"Oh…." Shuey looked around as he thought about it. "Are there no short fathers? There are. I know. But you're right that most of them are not so short." He scanned the room for something that could help him grow quickly.

"Besides," Bentzy added mercilessly, "how will it look to have a father with a yellow-and-green plaid shirt with green pants?! Everyone will laugh at you."

"It really is too bad that I don't have my Shabbos clothes here," Shuey said regretfully. "Black pants and a white shirt. That's all I need."

"And something to make you taller."

Shuey looked around again, and then saw the brooms resting near the door of the laundry room. "I can't stand on a broom, right?" he sighed with disappointment.

"Because if I could stand on the two sticks, and walk, then I'll be tall enough."

"So how will you dress up?" Bentzy kept asking. "With what?"

"Let's see what Aunt Chana has in her toy boxes," Shuey tugged at Tully's hand. "Maybe we'll find something there to dress up with. We'll also look for something to make me taller."

"What, like a magic powder to make us grow?" Tully's eyes glittered as he imagined himself growing taller and taller.

"No," Shuey cut off his fantasy. "Something that I can stand on, that's not too tall or too short, and comfortable."

"Let's go!"

## Chapter 4

# *Dressing Up!*

The three of them, Shuey, Bentzy, and Tully, ran up the stairs to the last room. They called it that for the simple reason that it was the last room in Aunt Chana's house. It was on the top floor, and the roof was slanted, like an attic. This room enchanted the children more than any other. It wasn't because of the gorgeous scenery: the sea, with its crashing waves could be seen from the little window. It was the toys that caught the children's attention. This was Aunt Chana's playroom. She had bought lots of toys, carpeted the room, and turned it into a real playroom. The children enjoyed spending time in this room made just for them. It really was any child's dream come true.

Now they went up to the room, taking the stairs two at a time. They burst inside and began rummaging for accessories that they could use.

"A costume box!" Shuey crowed, not believing his good luck. "Do you remember that we got dressed up the first day we came here?!" He turned the box over and various costume items that their aunt had accumulated over the years fell onto the floor.

"How is a gorilla mask going to help us?" Tully asked dejectedly. He fingered the smelly rubber and brought the dreadful mask to his face. "Grrrr! Oooohhh! I'm not afraid of you!" The gorilla with the scary teeth did not look offended.

"I don't like such scary masks at all." Tully tossed it away. "Besides, it would scare the little kids at the fair."

"Good, because it's useless for us. We can't go to the fair with the false identity of a gorilla!"

"Why not?" Bentzy brightened. "Of course we can! We'll dress up as a gorilla and we'll make a show!"

"*We'll* dress up? I thought you're not coming!"

"*You'll* get dressed up," Bentzy emphasized as he put his goody-goody expression back on his face. "I am really not going."

"Look! Mordechai HaYehudi's beard!" Shuey exclaimed, pressing the long white beard to his face with the help of the elastic string. "Now I really look old! And it's even better than looking young, because old men are shorter than young ones."

"Can't be!" Tully had a look of disbelief on his face. "What? Old people shrink like children grow taller?"

"Yes, it seems that way," Shuey said. "Because look — Abba is taller than Saba Rubinstein."

"That means nothing," Tully objected. "He could have always been taller."

"What, he was also taller when he was a boy?" Tully imagined a very tall boy indeed, even taller than his father and the *rebbi*. "Imagine that *Rebbi* would ask the boy to take things down from a high place, or to write the heading on the board—"

"No, you funny kid! I mean when they were both young men."

"I'm not funny!"

"But you don't understand!"

"Because it can't be!"

A heated argument broke out. Was it possible that an older man reached a certain age and started to get shorter? Bentzy hushed the argument.

"I thought you want to go already. Soon it will be night and the fair will close. And you won't be able to go."

The argument fizzled out. The boys began discussing the different items they found. Could they wear a white beard and dress up as an old man? Or maybe it would be better to wear just a mustache and dress up as a young *bochur*? They decided that the question of their height — or lack of it — would be decided later.

"You know what?" Bentzy suddenly said after deciding that one of them would dress up as an old man and the other would be a *bochur*.

"What?"

"You can just go dressed as children."

"Why?" Tully asked. He was very disappointed; he really wanted to be an old grandfather.

"Because this fair is not for old people or fathers. It's for mothers and girls and boys up to age nine!"

The boys exchanged glances. Bentzy had a point.

"So we should dress up as children?" Shuey sounded annoyed. "What kind of costume is that?"

"Yes, it's the simplest," Bentzy said practically. "Just dress up as a different boy! Someone who you don't even know! You don't even have to know his name!"

Shuey looked at his brother in admiration. There was a spark of brilliance to his words. There was no need to change clothes! The height would also be fine, and their problems would be solved! "It's an idea," he said. "I'll just dress up as a different boy!"

"And what about me?" asked Tully, the one who'd had the idea in the first place. "Will I also be a different boy?"

"Yes! We can decide, each one of us, which different boy he is, and this way we'll be with false identities and we can go to the fair!"

"So I'll dress up as you!" Tully had another idea from his endless supply. "And you'll be me!"

"Dress up as you?" Shuey studied his brother uneasily. "How can I dress up as you? We're wearing the same clothes!"

They looked at each other carefully. "Even our hair is the same color," Shuey complained. "How can you dress up as someone who looks almost exactly the same as you?"

"The shoes!" Bentzy announced. "Your shoes are not the same!"

"So we'll change shoes?" Shuey asked, a note of hesitation creeping into his voice.

"Yeah!"

They both took off their shoes. Tully didn't have such a problem. Shuey's shoes were bigger than his, but they were spacious and comfortable for him. Shuey was the one who had to curl up his toes so he could stuff his foot into Tully's shoes. After all, Tully was two years younger.

"Ugh…" he grumbled. "What tiny shoes you have, Tully. I can't get into them!"

"I have no problem getting into them," Tully sniffed. "Just squeeze your feet a little and you'll see they'll be comfortable for you as well."

Shuey squeezed and curled, as Tully had said, but it was impossible to say he was comfortable. His toes rubbed hard against his younger brother's shoes. "Ouch…. ugh…" he groaned. "It's tight. And it hurts."

"Don't complain," Tully said sternly. "Now — off we go!"

## Chapter 5

# *Shoe Problems*

"Wait," Bentzy said before his brother began to walk. "But you're not really going to the fair!"

"Why not?" Tully asked. "I'm not me, and Shuey is not Shuey!"

"Right," Bentzy agreed. "But if you're Shuey and Shuey is you, then it doesn't change anything!"

"Why?" They both stared at him.

"Because," Bentzy said studiously, "Tully is not allowed to go to the fair, and neither is Shuey. So what did you get out of this whole switch?"

There was a long silence while the two tried, with great effort, to resolve this latest problem. Mind you, Bentzy didn't say what he said just to be helpful. Really he didn't want to be left out while his brothers went out and had a good time. That was one thing. The other thing was that he was feeling very guilty. The idea of going out to the sea had been his, and since then, he'd been making every effort to be on his best behavior.

"Fine," Shuey said with a long sigh. "So we won't go."

"What?!" Tully was shocked. "After all this time we spent getting ready!"

"So we'll go just to say what it's like to go out dressed up," Shuey offered a compromise. "But we won't actually go to the fair."

Tully thought this idea over. It wasn't perfect, because the whole point was to go to the fair. But he also agreed that it wasn't really a solution to switch identities with his brother and to disobey their mother. Going dressed up was a quarter of the fun, even if not half. "Fine," he said with a resigned sigh, "we'll just *try* to go dressed up, but not really…."

And so, the two set out, accompanied by Bentzy's advice and good wishes. Personally Bentzy didn't think it would be very pleasant to go out in shoes that were either too big or too small on him. But no one had asked him about that.

They two began to walk, and very quickly realized that it was no fun at all.

"Ouch, your shoes are so tight," Shuey grumbled.

"Stop saying that already!" Tully rolled his eyes. "Look at me! Every second, the shoe flies off, and I have to run after it. And I'm not complaining as much as you are!"

"It's much better to chase shoes than to squish your toes like this," Shuey groaned. "In the end, my toes are going to bleed!" he added as a warning, as if he were threatening an earthquake.

"Put on a Band-Aid." Tully was unmoved by the threat.

"Is that how you care about your brother?" Shuey could not believe his ears. "I'm telling you that I'm suffering and you ignore me?"

Tully didn't answer. He had to run ahead after the shoe that had flown off his foot again. He didn't have any more time to listen to his brother's problems.

And so, the two of them hobbled ahead, looking more like a pair of ducks than two children. Their strange gait was because Shuey was suffering from the too-small shoes that belonged to Tully, while Tully was busy running after Shuey's too big shoes. Ayala, who had come to Aunt Chana's house to watch her younger brothers, and to make sure they didn't get into any mischief, spotted them from the window. To her surprise, she saw her two brothers leaving the house. Before she could call them, she noticed that they were limping along, and wondered what was going on. After taking a closer look she realized: they had switched shoes with one another! Why? She had no idea, and could not figure out what the two boys were up to. What would make two regular boys switch shoes?! It did not seem like Tully was hiding anything in Shuey's shoes because she could see them flying and flipping over so many times, that if there was something inside, it would have long fallen out.

"*Nu*, come on already," Shuey called to his brother, when Tully lagged behind again because of his too-big shoes. "The fair is going to finish soon and we won't get there because you're going so slow!"

Ayala didn't hear the whole sentence, because she was far away, but she did pick up the words "fair," "get there," and "going" and she got very angry. These two boys were going against what Ima and Aunt Chana had said! This was not just mischief; this was real chutzpah! How dare they? As mischievous as they usually were, they were not usually chutzpadik and disobedient of their parents. They always had a reason, an excuse, a claim about why they had done what they had done. Their intentions were always good. And now what? They had heard that Ima had forbidden them to go to the fair, and they were going anyway!

Before she'd take any further action, Ayala decided she had to get to the bottom of this. She could only do that after she saw that they were really going to the fair without any other intention, such as, for example, bringing Aunt Chana something she'd forgotten. Or giving Shevi her glasses or Etty her wallet.

Their hands were empty, so it wasn't likely that they were going to bring something to the girls. But all she knew about those boys right now is that they were heading for the fair. She needed more solid proof.

She slipped out the front door, walking cautiously, trying to hide behind trees whenever possible. Although, she thought, even if she'd break out in a dance in the middle of the street, the two boys would not notice her. They were so busy with their shoes (Why in the world had they changed shoes?! She was stumped!) that they did not notice anything else going on around them. She'd wait and see what this strange behavior was all about….

## Chapter 6

### *Water and Mud*

Shuey decided to put an end to his unbearable suffering, and he began to run toward their unclear destination (the fair?) as Tully, struggling to keep his shoes on, lagged behind.

"Hey, hey, what are you running for?" Tully tried to catch up with his brother as one shoe flew ahead and another one fell behind. "I can't run with these shoes!"

"So squeeze your toes and try to keep the shoes on with your toes," Shuey suggested. He didn't want to wait for his younger brother when his own feet were feeling so pinched.

"I'm squeezing and squeezing," Tully was offended. "I thought about doing that already...but it doesn't help!" He was breathless now. "And it's taking double the time, because I run forward to pick up the shoe that flew ahead. Then I have to go back to get the shoe that stayed behind….." As he spoke, one shoe flew off and hit Shuey in the back.

"Ouch!" Shuey screamed. "Why did you throw a shoe at me?"

"I didn't throw it! It flew by itself! I told you that—"

"Yes, yes, yes." Shuey nodded impatiently. "Just come on already!"

"I'm coming," Tully panted, holding one of the shoes in his hand, as he tried to fix the other. Walking like this — with one foot bare — he suddenly gave a little shriek: "Ouch…I think a thorn got into my foot!"

"That's all we need now!" Shuey muttered. "A thorn? Where?"

"Here." Tully pointed to his aching foot. "Look." Indeed, a tiny dot of blood appeared on his left big toe through his white sock.

"If it's bleeding that's a sign the thorn is out already," Shuey said wisely. "That's what Ima always says. If the thorn was inside, the blood would not be able to come out. Maybe there was a thorn, but it's out. And don't walk barefoot again."

"Am I to blame for being barefoot? I took one step with the shoe and then it fell off. I had to put my foot somewhere."

"Where?!" Shuey asked. "Why didn't you put it on the sidewalk, plain and simple?"

"Yes, I put it on the sidewalk, and that's why the thorn got stuck," Tully tried to explain.

"So you didn't put your foot just someplace, you put it on the sidewalk."

"I have to rest now," Tully declared. "I'm tired and my foot hurts!" He looked around. They were walking on the sidewalk. To their left was a small park, with a metal bench affixed to the ground in front of it. "Oh, here's a bench," he said as he sighed with relief and limped toward it. "Now I'm resting here!"

The two hurried toward the bench. "Ugh…there's lots of mud here," Shuey muttered. "I wonder where all this mud comes from." They didn't know that there was a water sprinkler right nearby, aimed at the bushes.

"*Oy vey*! Stop!" Shuey cried. Tully stopped quickly, but his shoes, which refused to stop, flew off his feet. One fell onto the bush and the other, onto Shuey's head.

"What's this? Help! A bird! Something fell on me! A cat!"

"It's not a bird," Tully said, as his feet sank into the mud. "And it's not a cat either. It's just a shoe." He took the shoe off his brother's head. "And why did you scream 'Stop!'? Because I stopped so fast both shoes flew off. And now I'm stuck in the mud!"

"So get out of the mud, and come already!"

They hurried to the bench, but the sprinkler, which was working at full speed, showered them both with lots of water.

"Wowow!" Tully choked back a scream.

Shuey hushed him. "Shhhhh…."

"I'm all wet," Tully protested.

"So am I! But don't scream like that! It's a *chillul Hashem*! You don't scream in the street!"

At that moment, the sprinkler showered them again with another round of cold water. This time, neither of them could hold back and they cried: "Brrrrr!"

Ayala crossed the street on the way to her brothers. She felt that there was no valid excuse for what they were doing, although Tully's strange dance — back and forth, forth and back — because of his shoes, brought a smile to her face. And Shuey, too, who was taking quick steps because he just wanted to get rid of his shoes, didn't make her laugh, but rather brought another small smile to her face. They looked so funny, how could she not smile a little? But most of all she was angry at her little brothers. How could they not listen to Ima like that?!

Now they were both sitting on the bench, and didn't look at all guilty. When they saw her, they hurried over to her happily. "Ayala! Look what happened to me!" Tully cried.

"And my foot hurts!" Shuey added.

"Where did you go?" she demanded.

"We wanted to go to the fair," Shuey began to explain.

"To the fair?!" Ayala echoed angrily. "Didn't Ima tell you that you're not allowed to go?"

"But we wanted to go under a false identity!" Tully said defensively.

"What? You wanted to go how?" She didn't understand.

"We thought we could go," Shuey repeated, "with a

false identity. Each one of us had the false identity of someone else!"

"But then Bentzy said that also wasn't good," Tully continued. "So we decided just to dress up and see how it is to be under a false identity…. It's not interesting at all! And it's also very hard to switch shoes…and I got a thorn in my foot…and Shuey said that he's—"

"And Tully couldn't—"

"And it happened because of you—"

"And the sprinkler—"

Ayala decided to hush them both. "Come home," she said and then sighed. "I'm glad you can tell that sometimes, your ideas are not all that great!"

Shuey glowed with pride. "So you're also saying that lots of times they *are* great!"

## Chapter 7

### The Raffle

"Would you have believed that she could make an entire family just out of balloons?" Shevi could not get over it.

Riki looked at the woman with admiration. In contrast to Shevi, she didn't just want to watch. In her active imagination she was already picturing herself blowing up balloons and designing them as she liked. Even imagining making a briefcase of balloons and then taking it to school…. That would be so nice. She would slide her Chumash notebook into the balloon-case… and her Yahadus notebook. It would be a bit squishy for the math notebook, but—

"Riki!" Shevi shook her shoulder.

With a sigh, Riki shrugged off her dream. When she put in her math book, the briefcase would probably bust from the weight. Oh well....

"Riki!" Her sister shook her again.

"Huh? What?"

"Look how nice!" Shevi was excited by a little baby with a blue pacifier in his mouth and large round eyes. "Look at this baby! He's made of balloons!"

"Maybe we can take one home?" Riki hoped aloud.

"How can we take one? It probably costs lots of money." Shevi felt her pockets, because she'd stuck ten shekels into one of them in case she'd need something. "More than these ten silly shekels."

Riki's eyes still gazed half-dreamily at the creation. "It's so beautiful!"

Shevi looked at her sister's hopeful expression and made a decision.

When the activity was over, they left to go search for their sisters and hear about the activity they had enjoyed. The meeting with Miri and Chani was animated, as they excitedly traded experiences. When they finished describing what they had each done, they began to look for Etty and Lali.

They made a round of the tents, but didn't find the two until they reached the raffle tent. Lali was sitting rooted to her spot. She refused to move, in case someone else came. And Etty was sitting next to her, looking desperate. Her eyes lit up when she saw her four sisters approaching.

"We've been here for twenty minutes already," she told them. "Lali doesn't want to move. She put tickets into the raffle and then said Tehillim. Now she says she has to win, and she won't leave here until she does."

"You won't lose the prize if you're not in the tent when they call out the winners," Riki explained reasonably. "Why should you sit here for another half hour?"

"Not half an hour," Lali pointed to the schedule in her hand. "The raffle is in ten minutes. I told Etty she could go."

"I'll stay with her," Shevi volunteered. "Go to a different tent, Etty."

"We were at the snake tent already. Lali held a snake that's five feet long!" Etty described dramatically.

"Don't exaggerate," Lali chided her. "He wasn't five feet long…but he was pretty long…." she admitted.

"Whoever wants to go look at all the stuff at the fair, can go. I'm staying here."

Etty hurried out with the other girls. Shevi, who had volunteered to stay with Lali, sat down next to her younger sister. "Which raffle did you enter?" she asked curiously. But Lali's face took on a look of secrecy. "Wait and see," she whispered.

The fair came to an end and all the girls gathered from all ends of the promenade-fairground and sat down on the benches in the raffle tent. Of the Schneider girls, only Lali and her faithful companion, Shevi, got to sit in the first row. Aunt Chana, who came into the tent last, received a seat of honor from the organizers, so she also sat next to the girls in the front row.

"Now, for the grand raffle," the emcee announced.

Shevi tensed. Is this what Lali had meant? But Lali looked rather calm and quiet. Only her eyes, gazing at one box, shone with excitement.

"First up is the mountain bike," the emcee announced. Silence fell on the tent, and a young girl, who was shorter than the bike, came away with the prize. "It's for my brother," she told those around her.

"Next!" the emcee called in that same excited tone. "A fashionable tote bag!"

Lali's expression was bored. "A bag, really," she scoffed. "Who needs such a thing? You can put your notebooks in a shopping bag. Why waste ten shekels for a raffle ticket on that?"

"Now — the surprise!" the emcee crowed. The worker dragged a wrapped box that wobbled a bit. "This is a donation from 'The Animal Corner'!"

Lali's eyes opened wide and her body leaned forward tensely. Her lips moved as she davened fervently. Strange noises were coming from the box. Someone was pushing the box from inside. It was very suspicious, because bags and toys and books do not move the boxes in which they are found.

"The winner is…Leah Schneider!"

"I won!!!" Lali shrieked joyfully. "I won!!! I won!!!"

"Of course," the emcee's assistant added in a scornful tone, "no one else entered this raffle besides you."

"What's in there?" Aunt Chana approached with Lali, who was literally skipping at her side. She was very suspicious.

"What's in the box?" She hadn't been in the raffle tent, so she hadn't studied the list of prizes up for grabs in the Chinese auction. There were no watches or necklaces here; these were prizes that interested children: a bike, cute sheet sets, various toys, decorative items, and more. The only box, Chana had noticed, that was closed on all sides was this one. Now the top was open, and she could peek inside at the prize.

"A lamb!!!" Lali shrieked. "I won the lamb!!"

Chapter 8

## A Little Lamb

Aunt Chana gaped at the child. "You entered the raffle for this creature?"

The box opened, and an innocent little fuzzy lamb, trembling on her thin legs, emerged for all to see. The audience stared in shock.

"Yes, she was standing there on the side, in the box, and could barely see what was going on outside! I felt bad for her and decided that I was going to win her."

"Who gave this idea to the fair organizers?!" Aunt Chana stared very sternly at the cheerful emcee, who continued reading out the names of the other winners. The emcee did not return her gaze. She was too busy. And what did she care? She's wasn't the one who now had to deal with a baby lamb!

"I don't know," Lali answered the question that Aunt Chana had asked the emcee. "But it's a wonderful idea, isn't it?!"

"Wonderful?! Wonderful?!" Aunt Chana looked around helplessly. "You don't mean that we should take her home?!" She tried to hide her horror.

"Why not?" Lali asked. "Why did I put in the ticket? Oy, look how scared she is…." Lali put out her hand, and tore the box to pieces. The lamb stepped out of the prison that she had been placed in, and stepped onto firmer ground.

Lali bent over to her. "You're so cute," she said softly. "And I'll take care of everything you need."

"How do you *know* what it needs?" Etty asked. She was the least stunned of all the sisters. The rest were shocked into silence. "You don't know what sheep need."

"I spoke to the owner of the farm. He's the one who brought the snakes. Besides, I know everything about animals perfectly. See? Now she's afraid and I have to calm her down."

The lamb raised her head and emitted a clear "Baaa…"

Aunt Chana remained rooted to her place in shock. "What-who-how…." she stammered. Then she sank onto the nearest bench, weak-kneed. "Lali, what are you going to do with this lamb?"

"What do you mean? I'm going to take her home. She'll live in your house for a few days and the day after tomorrow we are going home. I hope that Nita isn't also allergic to lambs."

"Maybe Nita isn't allergic, but I am." Aunt Chana tried to regain control of the situation. "She cannot come into my house."

"So I'll leave her outside," Lali reassured her aunt. "She'll eat grass, and she'll love it. You have lots of grass in the yard, Aunt Chana."

"*Hashem yishmor.*" Aunt Chana leaned back on the bench, her face as white as…lamb's wool. "What will you do afterwards? Will your mother let you bring this lamb home?"

"Sure!" Lali answered brightly. "It's a *kosher* animal! My father always said that we can't have *tamei* animals in our house. But a lamb used to be brought as a *korban* in the Beis Hamikdash!"

"Lali." Miri finally found her tongue, and her voice was sharp and decisive. "Ima will not let you raise a lamb in our house. We have twenty-one children, *baruch Hashem.* Our house is full enough."

"That's right," Chani joined in. "If Hashem would send us a baby girl we would be willing to crowd for her," Chani said. "But for a baby lamb? No. No. There is no reason we should, and it makes no sense, and no normal person would let you take this lamb home."

"*You* won't decide for me!" Lali retorted, and looked to Etty as an ally. "We'll wait for Ima to come home."

"No. I'll tell her what I think on the phone," Shevi cried in disgust, as she ran away from the lamb's little pink tongue that was trying to lick her. "Help! She's chasing me!"

"She's not chasing you. She's following you."

"I don't care what you call it!" Shevi climbed up on the bench. "Take it away from me!"

"She likes you, that's all." Lali took the confused little sheep, which began to wander among the benches that were growing emptier every minute. "That's why she's following you. She wants to be your friend."

"I don't want friends like her!" Shevi cried from her perch on the bench. "Oy! She's still coming! Lali! Take this thing away from me!"

The lamb was wandering among the benches. She tried to walk forward, and butted her head on the wooden bench. She walked backwards and knocked over a pile of plastic chairs with a loud clatter. There was almost no one left, except the Schneider girls, Aunt Chana, and the lamb of course. As she made her way to freedom, the lamb's head bumped into a plastic chair and she bleated pitifully.

Lali looped a thin rope around the small lamb's neck and led her among the chairs outside of the tent. Now they were all standing outside, talking in a babble.

"There's nothing to discuss—"

"Why not? It'll be nice—"

"You would say that!"

"And meanwhile think of how Aunt Chana will suffer from—"

"And how can we—"

"Missus!" The cleaning worker turned to Aunt Chana impatiently, and with a strong Arabic accent. "Why are you still standing here? We're cleaning up. You need to leave fast."

"But the lamb…it's not…I mean why…the lamb…." Aunt Chana stammered.

"First take her from here," the worker said, and began to drag the busted box. "Then talk to the owners of this mess to take her back."

Aunt Chana groaned. Who was going to help her out now?!

Lali was jumping around like a bunny; she was too happy to even talk. "A lamb! A lamb! A lamb!"

"Oh, the child is so happy," Aunt Chana murmured in despair. "I don't have the heart to disappoint her!"

## Chapter 9

# *Homes Are for Humans*

On the way home, Lali could not stop dancing and skipping. She led the little lamb at the head of their procession, like a queen presiding over her loyal subjects. She did not understand the meaning of the thoughtful expressions on her sisters' faces. In her mind, it was clear that this sweet little lamb would be joining their family. After all, Chevy had just gotten married, so now there was room for it!

Not that she thought the sheep would sleep in Chevy's bed (although that wasn't a bad idea at all! The question was if Ayala would be as excited as Lali was. For some reason, she didn't think Ayala would welcome the lamb into the other bed in her room), but the fact that the Schneiders now had one less child under their roof surely meant that Lali could fill that space with her new pet raffle prize.

"Do you think Aunt Chana will agree to host the lamb for two days?" Etty whispered to her.

Lali looked at her innocently. "Why not? You see how many children she agreed to take in. Why shouldn't she want to do *hachnasas orchim* for a lamb, too?"

"Because," Etty said what was clear to her, but not at all to Lali, "there's a big difference between a lamb and a person."

"Of course," Lali agreed with that. "There's a difference. But because of that difference someone won't agree to let a lamb live in his house? I'd be very surprised!" Lali liked to speak in an adult-like fashion.

"Yes," Etty answered, in mature language. "Because of this difference between a person and an animal, people want to live in homes built for humans, and they refuse to raise farm animals in their house."

"Well, Aunt Chana didn't say anything," Lali replied with a shrug of her shoulders. "I took the lamb with me and she didn't say a word."

"Maybe because she couldn't even get the words out? Or because you didn't give her a chance?"

"I'm not the one who has to give her a chance," Lali said, sounding a touch impatient. Lali was tired, and deep down, she was worried about her parents' reaction to the cute lamb. Could she part from it?! No way. That was not something to even think about, certainly not if she had any say in the matter. She'd need to find a solution. An explanation. A possibility. Where would the lamb live? That wasn't a problem. On the roof! Yes! Not in Yoni's dovecote. But there *was* room up there for a small pen for a lamb. True, it would take up more space and she'd also have to let the lamb out every day to let walk around freely, but it was possible! For sure it could work! Lali angrily shook her head at her imaginary opponents. She had to come up with persuasive arguments to prove just how right she was.

"…yours." Etty concluded what must have been a long and impressive speech, because she looked at Lali expectantly, as if she was waiting for a big compliment.

"I didn't hear a word," Lali admitted.

"I said," Etty said, a bit hurt, "that Aunt Chana *did* tell you that she's not sure she'll agree to—"

"Enough!" Lali had tried not to show her impatience. But now it was out in the open. "She didn't tell me 'no' and that's enough for me. There are people who, for some reason, don't like animals. Aren't they strange?"

"No, they are right in their way," Etty argued as she opened the iron gate of Aunt Chana's villa.

Standing at the entrance was Chavatzelet, smiling. "So? Did you enjoy the fair?" The smile faded from her face as she saw the procession from up close.

"And what is this?" she demanded to know.

"A lamb," Lali answered innocently.

"What???"

"A lamb, and it's not even one year old," Lali repeated.

"What???"

"A little lamb." Lali didn't tire of repeating herself.

"Yes-yes-yes," the cook stammered, pale-faced. "And what is it doing here, this one-year-old lamb?"

"It's not yet one year old," Lali corrected her. "That's what the man from the farm told me."

"The man from the farm? What is his name?"

Lali shrugged and stuck out her bottom lip. "Dunno. Why does it matter? I'll give the lamb a name myself."

She started to walk, as if to lead the lamb through the gate.

"What?!" Chavatzelet gave a strangled cry. "You...you... you...are g-g-going to bring that...that...thing into this house?"

"Sure!" Lali said warmly. "What did you think? That I'd leave her outside? She's *my* lamb! Outside, she might catch a cold, or she could get attacked by wolves, or she could be stolen or get lost!"

"There's nothing to worry about," Chavatzelet said darkly. "I don't see any predictions for a cold spell in this area. There are no wolves wandering around here, and most importantly: no one will steal her. No one would bring such a thing into his house, except for that Yid who had a big family."

"Which Yid?" Lali was curious. There was someone else who thought like her and brought a lamb into the house?!

"A Yid once came to his *rav*'s house," Chavatzelet related. "He told the *rav* how hard things were. He had ten children, *bli ayin hara,* in a small, one room apartment. There was no room. The overcrowding was driving him out of his mind. What did the *rav* say? 'Do you have a goat?' The man answered that he did. The *rav* said to him, 'Bring it into the house to live with you in the room.'"

"What?" Lali gasped. "But that would make it even more crowded!"

"That's right," the cook said. "A week later, the Jew came back to the *rav*, sobbing. The goat was dirty and noisy and was making it impossible to live there, so the wise *rav* told him: 'Good, now you can take the goat out.' The Yid did as he was told, and what did he discover? That his tiny house was now so roomy. Because after the goat was gone, it was spacious and neat compared to the way it had been with the goat inside…."

"Oh, thank you so much," Lali said brightly. "I bet that is *exactly* how Aunt Chana will feel after this lamb moves out!" And with that, Lali led the lamb right past the misunderstood cook and right into the front yard.

## Chapter 10

### Grazing in the Garden

"What could I have done?" Aunt Chana asked helplessly. "The child was so thrilled."

"I'm not telling you what to do, of course," Chavatzelet said. "But the child's mother will be a lot less thrilled."

"That's for sure," Aunt Chana groaned. "But I'm not a mother, and my heart just didn't let me tell her *not* to take the lamb with her! It also would have been *tza'ar baalei chaim* to leave it there."

"Why?"

"Because no one there planned to take care of it. Everyone had already packed up their stuff and left. No one would have looked after a small, lost lamb."

"Small?" Chavatzelet peeked out through the window,

where the lamb was frolicking on the grass, and near the flowers. She looked very big compared to the little creatures that had lived in the garden until now. "It's not so small…. And lost? Maybe. A bit…."

"So we took her, with a bag of food for her." Aunt Chana placed the bag on the table. "Although I think it's better to buy her sheep's milk. It's what a lamb her age should be eating."

"Cow's milk won't be good enough?" Chavatzelet glanced again at the animal, which, every so often, stuck out her pink tongue and bleated, "Maaaaaa!"

"Aren't you afraid she'll ruin the flowers?" Chavatzelet asked after a moment of silence.

"I hope she won't." Aunt Chana wasn't sure about the lamb and how to care for it, so she thought it was important to be doubly careful. She could always ask the gardener to plant new flowers. But the lamb did look, somehow, like something whose needs needed to be taken into consideration. "In any case, she's one level above a plant," she apologized when she saw Chavatzelet's shocked face. The cook knew how much Aunt Chana loved the plants and flowers in her garden. "She is part of the animal group, which is superior to the plant group."

"And then there's the level of the *medaber,* one who speaks," the cook harrumphed. "Like me, for example."

"Does it bother you that she's grazing in our garden?"

"I'll only go out from the back door," Chavatzelet decided. "Just don't ask me to feed her or anything."

"No, we have Lali for that. She'll take care of the lamb on her own. I don't think there will be any other volunteers."

"One of her sisters will probably offer to help, the one with the short hair." She was referring to Etty.

"Could be," Aunt Chana nodded. There was an expression on her face that was hard to decipher. "But neither one of us."

Again Aunt Chana glanced at the window. The lamb didn't look so quiet just then. She stood up from where she had been sitting and paced up and down the garden. Chavatzelet joined Aunt Chana in watching. They both watched the little animal uneasily.

"What does she want?" Chavatzelet finally asked.

"Do I know?" Aunt Chana answered with a sigh. "Do I look like a veterinarian?"

Again they gazed at the lamb, which was walking back

and forth, back and forth. Every so often, she raised her voice with a loud "Meh!!"

The two women exchanged glances. "Is this how every lamb acts?" Aunt Chana asked Chavatzelet doubtfully. "Or is she just not happy? Or lonely?"

"Why shouldn't she be lonely?" Chavatzelet's conscience began to niggle at her. "Walking there alone, a little lamb in a big yard...alone in Hashem's huge world...Lost without a father or mother, without any friends...."

Aunt Chana swallowed a smile. "I didn't know you were poetic, Chavatzelet."

"Ah, whose heart does not flutter at seeing this lonely creature?" she added dramatically. "She does not know where she is going, and when she will arrive—"

"She actually knows very well where to go and where to come," Aunt Chana pointed out. "She is walking back and forth pretty nicely!"

As if in an answer to her words, the lamb stopped near the gate of the garden. She raised her head and looked at the gate with sad eyes, bleating loudly: "Meh! Meh! Meh!"

"What does she want?" Chavatzelet was near tears now.

"Maybe I should wake Lali up?" Chana mused aloud. "She said she'd take care of her lamb and I really don't know what the thing wants! She left her a plate with milk, but it looks like the poor lamb doesn't want to drink it."

"Maybe she misses her mother?" Chavatzelet whispered in a shaky voice.

"I don't know." Aunt Chana looked this way and that. Who could help them? "And if so? What should I do? I don't know her mother, and I don't know where to find her!"

"Even if you'd know who she is and where she is, you wouldn't be willing to bring her here!" Chavatzelet cried firmly. "One lamb living in this garden is terrible enough. But two? That would be a crisis that we couldn't handle! Two lambs bleating their annoying 'meh meh meh' the whole time?! What a tragedy!"

"Don't overdo it." Aunt Chana smiled tiredly. "It's not a tragedy. But yes, there is no doubt that I don't want to bring the mother here as well."

"Absolutely not!" Chavatzelet breathed a sigh of relief. She'd handle a little lamb somehow, but a big, scary mama sheep that would stand and stare at her threateningly?! No, no, no! She had come to Chana's home to be a cook, not a shepherd!

And yet, that night, she became exactly that.

## Chapter 11

### Shepherdesses

The lamb seemed to finish examining the garden. After she walked back and forth a few times, she stood next to the door and bleated a loud, "Meeehh!"

"Do you think…she wants to come inside?" Chavatzelet whispered in horror.

"Maybe," Aunt Chana said. Her face became stern. "But even if she wants to, I cannot fulfill her request."

"Oh," Chavatzelet sighed with relief. "And I thought that…I'd have to give up my place here…because she and I cannot be under the same roof."

"Look, look," the cook pointed breathlessly to the back part of the garden. "The door is open!"

"And so?" Aunt Chana asked. "It's usually like that. We

always leave it open, because the grocery man puts down the order there each morning."

"But the lamb," Chavatzelet choked out. "The lamb... it's...she's running away!"

And indeed she was. When the lamb got tired of wandering around the garden, she walked toward the gate. The entry gate was closed, so she dejectedly retraced her steps. But when she walked along the length of the fence, she noticed that there was another open gate, and it was calling her to freedom!

Without showing any excitement, acting as if this was totally normal behavior, the lamb began walking toward the open gate. Aunt Chana shrieked quietly. Chavatzelet's eyes were flitting around. With courage she didn't know she had, Aunt Chana grabbed a rolling pin and stepped out the front door to confront the fleeing lamb. Chavatzelet couldn't just stand there and do nothing. So she armed herself with the schnitzel hammer in one hand, and a ladle in the other, and followed Aunt Chana out to the garden.

The two stood side by side, not knowing what to do, and whom to turn to for help. The lamb had already stepped out of the open gate and begun to walk away.

"We need…" Aunt Chana swallowed, "to get her back home."

Chavatzelet couldn't say a word.

Aunt Chana courageously took one step forward.

Chavatzelet took a step back.

Aunt Chana got a tiny bit closer.

Chavatzelet couldn't just stand there, so she also took a teeny step closer.

"What should we do?" she asked Aunt Chana in an almost inaudible whisper. There were about six feet between them. Aunt Chana walked out of the gate, followed by Chavatzelet. In contrast to the two frightened, uncertain women, the lamb was decisive and cheerful. Her wail-like "meh-meh-meh" had stopped, and instead, she walked briskly toward…the unknown.

"She's about to cross the street," Aunt Chana said.

"That's dangerous," Chavatzelet agreed.

"We have to stop her."

"But the street is empty."

As you can see, neither of the women was brave enough to grab the lamb by the rope that was tied

around her neck, like Lali had done. If there had been cars on the road, Chavatzelet's sense of caution and Aunt Chana's sense of responsibility would have led them to grab the poor lamb, even if they were terrified. But the street was quiet and empty. It was a wealthy, upscale neighborhood, and most of the people were in their homes from eight in the evening. Now, it was already eleven.

The lamb looked very sure of herself. She crossed the street with a slight clip-clop of her hoofs. The silence on the street made it possible to hear the echo of her footsteps. Aunt Chana and Chavatzelet followed her, not knowing what they would be doing next.

The lamb, however, did know. She walked to the small garden flowering near the house across the street from Chana's house. She began enthusiastically gobbling up the flowers and the grass. The garden did not have a gate, and it didn't belong to a resident; it belonged to the city. But the neighbor who lived in the villa next door, old Mr. Kolbovitz, walked through the garden a lot, and enjoyed the flowers. He loved the garden.

"She's simply grazing in the meadow," Chavatzelet said almost to herself. They crossed the street after the lamb and stood a few steps away. They didn't know what to do. "Yes, yes, grazing in the pasture of the garden that Mr. Kalmanowitz loves so much."

"Kolbovitz," Aunt Chana corrected her, sounding a bit dejected.

"Whatever." Chavatzelet waved off the correction.

"She's eating the grass. Like a real lamb."

"Of course she's going to eat like a real lamb. What do you think she is, a toy lamb? Everyone can see she's real." And then she added a wish. "I wish she were a ceramic lamb, or a decorative lamb, or even a stuffed animal lamb!"

"She's a real lamb," Aunt Chana confirmed morosely.

"And I never thought," Chavatzelet murmured, "that I'd have to be a shepherdess."

"Yes," Aunt Chana said, because there was nothing else to say.

"I thought I'd cook lamb meat, but not that I'd have to deal with a real one," Chavatzelet continued.

"Lamb meat was once a real lamb," Aunt Chana commented, even though it really had nothing to do with anything.

Chavatzelet shuddered. The street light glowed above them and the lamb was still munching on the grass and flowers.

"What was wrong with your flowers, Mrs. Chana?" Chavatzelet demanded to know. "Why did she run so fast to Mr. Kalmanowitz's flowers?"

"Kolbovitz."

"Whatever."

## Chapter 12

# Mr. Kolbovitz Counts Sheep

Aunt Chana sounded tense. "We have to get her back home."

"Yes, yes," poor Chavatzelet answered. "Get her home!"

"But how?" Aunt Chana asked in despair.

"Yes, yes, how?" Chavatzelet echoed.

Aunt Chana sighed. She realized that she had to do something. The lamb could not stand here and chew Mr. Kolbovitz's flowers any longer! True, it was not his garden, but everyone knew that he loved it.

"Well," she said bravely, "we'll have to get her home." She was just repeating herself.

"Who? Just the two of us? Ourselves?" Chavatzelet did not see herself as suited to being a shepherdess.

"Do you see anyone else who can do this?"

Chavatzelet looked right, left and then right again. Forward, backward — and then she admitted, in distress, that there was no one suited for the job. Or more exactly — there was no one else there at all.

"So that's it," Aunt Chana said with resignation. "I'll walk behind the lamb and I'll try to…er…umm…push her forward slightly, so she'll walk. You'll stand in the front and guide her toward the gate."

"Who me?" Chavatzelet squeaked, and began to tremble like a bowl of soup on a tray. "Me?"

"Well, do *you* want to push the lamb from behind?" Aunt Chana suggested generously, concealing her smile.

"What, and touch it? No, no, no!" Chavatzelet cried.

"Fine, so I—" She coughed, "I, um, will go now." And she bravely walked toward the lamb. The little animal stopped eating and looked in surprise at the woman standing in front of her. "Meh!" she exclaimed loudly.

"Shhhh…quiet," Aunt Chana fretted. "You'll wake up Mr. Kolbovitz."

The lamb did not seem concerned about this at all, and just bleated again. "Meh-meh-meh!"

"Enough, enough," Aunt Chana groaned. "That's enough already. Do you want to wake up the whole neighborhood?"

"Meh!!" the lamb trumpeted loudly, as if that had been her plan from the very start.

Aunt Chana groaned again, and then gently patted the lamb's back. "Come, come." She swallowed, terrified. "Come to me...come to the field...I mean come to the garden." One couldn't exactly say that caring for sheep came naturally to her.

And on top of that the lamb was stubborn. She lowered her head, ignoring Aunt Chana, and emitted a quieter "Meh!" as if annoyed at having been disturbed. Then she went back to eating.

"What should I do?" Aunt Chana asked Chavatzelet. Aunt Chana's cook didn't know what to answer and just raised her hands as she shook her head sadly.

"Did you hear that, Ditza?" Mr. Kolbovitz listened closely. Despite being over eighty, he still heard well. His wife murmured something unclear.

"Didn't you hear that, Ditza?"

"I don't know what I have to hear. It's nighttime, Kalman. Go to sleep."

Kalman Kolbovitz, who was very proud of his interesting name, shook his head in disbelief. "I must have imagined it," he said, and put his head on the pillow.

Again he heard the noise, louder this time: "Meh-meh-meh!"

"I heard it!" He sat up in bed. "This time I heard it, I'm telling you!"

"What did you hear?"

"A lamb. I heard something bleating under the window."

"You counted sheep to fall asleep," she explained to him. "And you dream about what you think about right before bed. So you dreamed about a bleating lamb, that's all."

"I didn't count sheep," Kalman was offended. "Why would you think I counted sheep?"

"To fall asleep, of course," she soothed him. "There are people who count sheep. I like to count cats. They're softer, and also more inspiring."

"*Nu*, fine," Kalman said, only somewhat calmer. "But I didn't *count* sheep or cats. I *heard* a lamb."

"It's impossible," Ditza declared. "There's never been a lamb bleating in our neighborhood." What was true was true. Then again, the Schneider children had also never been in their neighborhood! And the minute a group of children like the Schneiders came, they were followed by lambs, elephants, lightning, and rooms painted black. There were also fish on the list.

"So, now a lamb is bleating for the first time," Kalman insisted. The silence in the street proved to him that he must be mistaken. But it was a mistaken proof. Ditza listened for another full minute before she lay down again. Then she shook her head doubtfully. "Change your hearing aids, Kalman. When I had problems with mine, I also started hearing sounds that weren't there. Turned out that there was something wrong with the device and I got it changed."

"Maybe," Kalman said. "But Ditza, I don't have hearing aids."

"Oh," his wife said. "Right. I forgot." One minute later, her head fell back on the pillow and she was asleep.

Kalman remained sitting up for one more minute. He didn't hear anything. *Ditza was probably right, and I just dreamed it*, he thought to himself. He was about to lie down again when he heard the sound of a lamb once again: "Meh!!!"

"That's it, this time it's real!" He threw off the blanket and walked over to the window. He heard the bleating. No one could tell him that he had counted sheep so he was dreaming about them!

He went to the front window, which faced the street. If anyone was pulling a silly trick on him, he would show them what he thought about it!

## Chapter 13

# Aunt Chana Makes a Decision (So Does the Lamb)

Mr. Kolbovitz looked this way and that. Everything seemed empty and quiet. He didn't turn his gaze to the garden on the street, in front of his house, beyond the gate to his private garden. That is why he didn't see the grazing lamb, or the two worried women who didn't know if they were coming or going.

"I didn't see anything," he murmured to himself as he got back into bed and covered himself with the blanket. "I won't tell Ditza," he told himself. "She'll say I dreamed about lambs again. But maybe I really did dream...I mean, I know that I didn't dream, but maybe it was a dream anyway? Because I didn't see anything...but I clearly heard the bleating of a lamb! And I have no issues with my hearing. On the contrary, I only wear glasses. *Nu*, but I didn't see anything…I did hear…."

A bit confused, he tried to fall asleep.

Just outside his house, things progressed very slowly.

"Come, little lamb, come," Aunt Chana tried to persuade the lamb to come with her. The lamb picked up her head, as if considering the idea, and emitted a belated "Meh!!" in objection to being disturbed. On the spur of a moment, she abandoned the garden and began walking toward the sidewalk.

When he heard the bleat, Kalman leaped out of his bed, tossed away the blanket and ran to the window. He rubbed his eyes over and over. Now he could see it clearly! A little lamb walking along the sidewalk! He rubbed his eyes again in disbelief. Could it be that he didn't only hear the sounds, he saw them too?!

Wait, but if the bleating was his imagination, this vision was not imaginary! Or were they both imaginary?! Was he dreaming about it all?! Or maybe it was all true?! Who could answer this puzzling riddle? If it was his imagination, then everything was resolved. And he would go back to bed and sleep peacefully. But if it was real, then strange things were happening and he needed help!

He hurried back to the room. "Ditza, Ditza, do you hear?" He woke his wife. "You have to see. Come, come, I saw her!"

"Who?" His wife's voice was very sleepy.

"The lamb!"

"Before you heard it and now you see it?" She was fully awake now, and looked at her husband worriedly. "Is everything alright, Kalman?"

"I don't know," he snapped. "Come and see for yourself!"

Concerned for her husband's welfare, and worried that at his age he had begun to imagine things, Ditza hurried to the window.

Meanwhile, Aunt Chana continued trying to be a shepherdess. She was very happy with the disciplined little lamb. Look! She had obeyed Aunt Chana's command and had left the garden! Now she saw herself as an excellent shepherdess! "Here, here, come here," she motioned. Chavatzelet handed her a stick from someplace, and she waved it in front of the lamb's face. The lamb looked rather scornful and turned to the other direction.

"You're going to the wrong side!" Aunt Chana called desperately.

"Maybe stop her?" Chavatzelet suggested from a safe distance away.

"How?"

"Stand in front of her and don't let her walk."

Aunt Chana was none too pleased with this idea. Imagine, she should stand and stop a very active lamb with her two hands! What if the lamb would lick her? Or bite? And if she'd push her with her head? Well, Aunt Chana was no bullfighter....

"Come back!!" Aunt Chana shouted on the quiet street.

"Don't scream for no reason," Chavatzelet advised. "She's a small lamb, and I'm sure that she's frightened by your screaming. She might also be offended."

"Where is that girl?" Aunt Chana groaned. She was exhausted by then. "In another minute the lamb will disappear! And then what will be?!"

"Where is the girl?" Chavatzelet replied innocently. "In the house, in her bed, sleeping deeply. Do you want me to go call her?"

"Of course!" Aunt Chana shouted, like someone drowning who sees a rescue boat approaching. "Why didn't we think of it until now? I'll stay here, and you run to call Lali!"

Chavatzelet turned on her heel and hurried toward the house.

"How come I didn't think of that?" Aunt Chana puzzled as she continued following the lamb. "We would have saved lots of time and effort...."

Lali was a bit confused when she was awakened. Chavatzelet's story about the lamb, the open gate, escape, flowers and bushes belonging to a Mr. Koblevitz or Kolbovitz but they actually belonged to the town — only mixed her up even more.

"What? What? What? What happened?" Lali kept asking.

"The lamb ran away," Chavatzelet started again. When Lali heard this, she shot out of bed, pulled on her robe and fumbled for her slippers. Within a minute she was in the yard, then the garden, and walking through the gate. Chavatzelet could hardly keep up with her.

"*Baruch Hashem*," Aunt Chana sighed when she saw the little figure striding quickly in her direction. Lali was trembling; despite the date — before Pesach — it was still very chilly outside, because Aunt Chana lived so close to the sea.

Lali didn't ask any questions. With a sure step, she bravely approached the lamb, put a hand on the rope tied around her neck and tugged it gently. The lamb, it seemed, breathed a sigh of relief. This little nighttime outing had confused her. She submissively let the little girl lead her back to the house.

Aunt Chana and Chavatzelet walked carefully behind Lali, their breathing much calmer now.

"This was a miracle," Aunt Chana sighed, "that you thought of that idea."

"Yes, yes," Chavatzelet affirmed her boss's words, as she usually did. "What would we do without this girl?"

"Very simple," Aunt Chana replied in a tone that was half serious and half humorous: "We wouldn't have won the raffle ticket for the lamb...."

## Chapter 14

# Mr. Kolbovitz Looks for Clues

"I didn't see anything." Ditza Kolbovitz closed the window. "Tomorrow we'll find out what happened."

"I saw a lamb, Ditza, I promise you." Kalman Kolbovitz was worried about becoming confused as he grew old. And this was exactly what he feared the most: imagining things that didn't exist. He had to find out what had happened or he would have no peace.

He got dressed, quickly and quietly putting on his lightweight coat and boots. He knew that the sprinkler worked at this hour and the ground was bound to be muddy. He took a flashlight and his walking stick and stepped carefully into his yard. He wouldn't tell anyone anything. If he found nothing suspicious, he'd just keep the secret to himself.

He walked out of the gate, flashlight in one hand, stick in the other. He was shaking a bit due to the cool breeze, and also because he was excited. He was about to uncover a major secret!

He turned to the place where he thought he had seen the small animal, and tried to find hoofprints.

But there were none. He saw no sign that an animal had walked here. He found no remnant of the nighttime "parade" of Lali, her precious lamb, Aunt Chana, and a trembling Chavatzelet, for they had all already made it back to Aunt Chana's house.

He shone his flashlight on the garden and stopped. Wait! There *were* footprints! *Clear ones*! Footprints of a person who had walked on the grass! He drew closer, and he could easily see the signs of the lamb's hoofs. One lamb had been here, and perhaps even more! The human footprints seemed to be going back and forth, and the animal's footprints also showed that it had walked back and forth. They must have been a lamb and a hesitant shepherd who couldn't decide whether he was coming or going.

Mr. Kolbovitz's guess was very close to the truth, as you know. But there was no shepherd, only a shepherdess —

and not one, but two or three. And the footsteps back and forth were the result of their fear, not their hesitation.

But Mr. Kolbovitz wasn't afraid. He was like a soldier on the battlefield! Like a detective at a crime scene! He shone his light on the bushes, and discovered the second major find of the night: The flowers had been chewed up! The bleating lamb that had woken him up had also gnawed at his flowers! That alone was already a crime! Hmm…. Could he sue the animal for damages? (He didn't know the laws about damages caused by animals, because he was a *tinok shenishbah*, a Yid who grew up without learning Torah. But he did think to himself that it would be very funny if the lamb would receive a formal letter saying, 'Dear Mr. Lamb, You are being taken to court for damage that you caused in my garden.' His past as a successful lawyer was coming back to life….)

In his mind, he was imagining showing up in court — with a lamb sitting next to him! Exactly what would the judge have to say about that? Wait a minute, he was getting mixed up. The lamb wouldn't be sitting next to him. *He was suing the lamb!* He would be sitting across from him, and would glare at him accusingly for suing in the first place….

Kalman Kolbovitz laughed out loud at his own vivid imagination, and enjoyed his late-night discovery. Tomorrow, he would knock at the door of the villa next door and try to find out if the owner knew anything about this mysterious lamb.

In the morning, everyone listened to the hair-raising tale told by Aunt Chana and Chavatzelet. Lali felt terrible about how frightened they had been, and what they had gone through, and didn't understand why they hadn't woken her up right away.

"I really didn't think this is what would happen, Aunt Chana." she began, and then stopped. Through the window in the front hallway, she saw a well-dressed man, wearing a fancy suit. He did not look *frum*, but he was knocking at their door. "Aunt Chana, someone is looking for you," she said.

The cook and Aunt Chana turned to see who it was, and they both gasped in alarm.

"Oh no," Aunt Chana murmured.

"Oh me, oh my," Chavatzelet said, and hurried to hide in the kitchen.

"What? Who?" Lali and Etty asked fearfully. "Who is this man?"

"That is Mr. Kolbovitz," Chavatzelet groaned as she bent over the deepest pot she found in the kitchen. "And yesterday, your lamb was munching away at *his* garden!"

"And what will happen now?" The girls were also afraid.

"Now? Now he's come here," Chavatzelet wailed. "He's probably come to ask about his garden!"

"I'll pay for the damages," Aunt Chana promised bravely. "Don't worry, girls."

Chavatzelet picked up her *sefer Tehillim*.

Etty was frozen in place.

Lali murmured *perek kuf lamed* — the only one she remembered by heart. *Shir Hama'alos mima'amakim….*

"Hello, Mr. Kolbovitz," Aunt Chana greeted the elderly neighbor.

"Oh, hello," he said distractedly. "I have an important question. Did you perhaps see a lamb last night?" There was a tense look in his eyes. Lali hoped the lamb was still in the back garden, and was not walking toward the front right now, incriminating herself. She had no sense, that animal, Lali thought angrily.

"Look, Mr. Kolbovitz, we'll pay any damage that was caused—" Aunt Chana began to say.

"But was there a lamb or not?!"

"Yes, there was a lamb," Aunt Chana tried to say. "Yes there was."

"There was?"

"Indeed."

"And it was grazing…in the garden near my house?"

"Yes, but—"

"Oh, thank goodness," Mr. Kolbovitz breathed a sigh of relief as he looked up toward the sky. "So there was a lamb! Wait till I tell Ditza! There was! And here I was worried that I'm imagining things!"

## Chapter 15

# *Home Sweet Home?*

"Are you sure," Aunt Chana asked Lali delicately, as Kobi loaded the lamb into his van, "that your mother is going to agree to keep this lamb?"

"Sure!" Lali declared. "She told me herself that if it's a kosher animal, there's no problem." The truth was not quite so clear cut, but Lali preferred not to think about it. Maybe once Ima saw how cute it was…. And besides, Abba had told her many times that non-kosher animals were not allowed into their home. So, if that was the case, then a kosher animal — and what was more kosher than a lamb that could be offered as a *korban* in the Beis Hamikdash?! — could be brought into their house….

Kobi looked rather amused. At first, Aunt Chana had deliberated whether to ask him about putting the lamb in his vehicle, because most normal people would not be very keen on having such fuzzy passengers. But Lali was shocked at the thought of separating her from her beloved lamb.

"If the lamb doesn't come in Kobi's van, how is it going to come?" she asked in horror. "She'll be very scared if she has to travel with strangers!"

When Kobi arrived, Aunt Chana shared the problem with him, very cautiously.

"Let's say," she said, "let's just say that someone asked you to take a...well an animal...in your car, from one place to another. Would you agree?"

"Are you talking about Lali's fish?" Kobi guessed right away.

"Actually not," Aunt Chana said miserably. "It's a one-year-old lamb."

Kobi's jaw dropped.

"Feel free to say no," Aunt Chana said hastily. "I don't mean, *chalilah*, to force you to take such a passenger if you're not comfortable with it."

"Umm," Kobi said, thinking hard. "Umm...."

"So, I understand you don't want to," Aunt Chana said, and her face took on a decisive expression. "I'll tell Lali right now that there's absolutely no way—"

"No, no, no," Kobi said quickly. "Don't tell her anything. I agree. But she'll have to watch the lamb during the ride."

"Are you sure?"

"Yes, it's fine," Kobi reassured her. "We'll manage."

And so it happened that at night, Kobi loaded the van with all the children's suitcases, and most of the children, and took them home. The next morning, all he had to do was take Etty, Lali, Miri, and their suitcases. And, let's not forget the lamb, of course.

The next morning, the girls said goodbye to Aunt Chana.

"It was amazing," Lali said warmly, in her typical open and cheerful way. "Thanks so much for everything! Especially for the lamb!"

"Thank you," Miri said in her mature tone. Etty smiled and said, "It was so nice here, Aunt Chana. Maybe we'll come again."

"I'm not sure she'll want that," Chavatzelet said with a crooked smile. "If you started with fish and continued with a lamb who knows what you'll bring next time? A dog? An elephant?"

"A lion," Lali said seriously. When she saw Chavatzelet's smile of disbelief, she told her about the story of the kitten and the lion. (You can read about it in *23 Under One Roof* volume 4 — *The New House*).

"Alright, alright." Chavatzelet felt like she needed a coffee. "Bye, kids!"

The girls went out to Kobi's van and settled themselves in. The suitcases were put in the trunk, and Lali sat down in the back seat. Then Etty placed the lamb on Lali's lap!

"That's it," she said, satisfied. "We can go!"

Miri and Etty sat down on the bench in front of Lali and the lamb, and the van set out.

And surprisingly enough, the trip was uneventful.

The boys were overjoyed when they found out that there was a guest of honor on the way. They had come home from Aunt Chana's house the night before, without having heard much about their sister having won a lamb. And when Kobi carefully unloaded the lamb from the back, Shuey, Bentzy, and Tully burst into excited cheering. They were so loud that some of the neighbors opened the windows to see what the fuss was about.

"Shhh! Quiet!" Lali chided them. "All the neighbors are going to come down!" She preferred that other people not see the lamb. She had a vague feeling that some of the neighbors would not understand the importance of raising a kosher animal, and they would demand that the lamb be sent back to wherever it came from. They also would not dance with joy when they'd hear, for example, that the lamb would be riding in the elevator that all the neighbors used. In short, there was a small chance that they wouldn't like her dear lamb....

"Let them come!" Bentzy crowed. "Let them see the signs we prepared for Abba and Ima!"

"But if they do, they'll also see the lamb," Lali whispered. "I don't want that to happen. Come, let's take her upstairs now."

Lali quickly led the lamb into the building. She looked around nervously, and pressed the button. She was not allowed to ride the elevator herself, so she waited impatiently for Miri to come. She knew there were a few more hurdles before she would be home free with this lamb. First she had to get her inside in peace, and then get her parents to agree. If the neighbors were against it, everything would be that much harder.

Miri finally came in and the lamb was put into the elevator. She apparently didn't like the crowded space, and every so often she raised her head and bleated, "Meh!" — sounding annoyed.

"Shhh…." Lali tried desperately to quiet her down. "If you talk too much the neighbors will come."

But no neighbor appeared, and Lali brought the lamb into the house and quickly shut the door behind them.

## Chapter 16

# Abba and Ima Come Home

"What the matter?" Abba noticed that Ima clicked to end the call and then dialed again.

"I got a wrong number," Ima said, sounding puzzled. "I don't understand how that happened. I mean, it's our home number…." She sighed again. She really wanted to go home already, to her darling children, and her blessed, daily routine.

She dialed again and listened. Abba watched her forehead crease and again, she hung up.

"Maybe you didn't make a mistake?" he suggested carefully.

"Can't be that I didn't make a mistake! I called and all I could hear was a sheep," Ima said. "I didn't call a farm.

That's how I know it was a mistake."

"A sheep?"

"Yes. You have to admit that our family is very interesting and colorful, but a sheep? Not part of the package!"

"Well, anything is possible," Abba said, concealing an amused smile under his mustache.

"No, not anything," Ima insisted. "There's a limit — even to what can happen in our house."

Abba shrugged. "You know what? Give me the phone."

Ima gave him the phone and said, "Sure, you try."

He dialed. He heard strange, muffled sounds from the other end, and then a voice said, "Hello?"

Abba breathed a sigh of relief. He recognized the voice as Etty's.

"Etty?" he asked, just to be sure.

Before Etty could reply, he heard another voice say, "Meh! Meh!"

A narrow crease, similar to the one that had been on Ima's forehead, crossed Abba's forehead. But unlike Ima, he didn't hang up so fast.

"*Nu?*" Ima asked.

"Wait." Abba felt like he needed all his wits about him to solve this mystery. "Who is this? Etty?"

Again he heard the bleating, and after that a whisper: "Pssssstttttffff...ccchchhhpppsss...ssss...pppsss...blblblb..." Then, a dial tone.

Abba gaped at the telephone in surprise.

"Didn't I tell you?" Ima asked triumphantly. "Something strange is going on there, right? Did you hear the bleating of a lamb?"

"Yes," Abba said as the crease in his forehead deepened. "But I also heard a lot of whispering, and Etty's voice."

"Do you think they're planning a surprise for us?" Ima was optimistic.

"Probably," Abba said, sounding worried. "But I have no idea what kind of surprise."

"It must be a recording of something," Ima decided. She hadn't heard all the suspicious whispering.

"Probably," Abba repeated.

He didn't say that the whispering sounded irritated, and then someone hung up on him. The hanging up was probably part of the whole thing, but still....

"The main thing is that we're back in Israel," Ima said, sighing happily. "I can't wait for the minute I see the kids!"

"Me, neither," Abba echoed. But something in his voice was still worried. The children would not have been so excited without good reason. And somehow, he had the feeling that whatever this reason was, it would not make Ima so happy at all.

"HHHEEEELLLOOOOO!" about ten children screamed as their parents walked in the door.

Ima tried to hug them all at once. Tzivi cried, and Ima picked her up. Then she picked up Eli and Tammy, and stroked Gila's face, pinched Tully's cheek, nodded at Bentzy, smiled as Shuey and said a thousand times, "yes, yes, yes," and "sure, sure, sure," and "hello, hello, hello."

Abba hugged Sruly, pinched a few of the children's cheeks, and laughed and cheered and picked them up and down and...then sank onto the couch, exhausted. Ima sat down across from him in the armchair. They were both glowing, exhausted, and thrilled. There were hand-drawn welcome signs hung all over the house, and all the children sat or stood around their parents.

Well, almost everyone. Through the fog of her exhaustion and excitement, Ima realized that someone was missing. Lali. That was not like her, unless there was a reason….

"Where is Lali?"

"She's preparing the surprise," Etty answered vaguely.

"Which surprise?"

"Surprise!" Lali announced from the doorway, in a slightly shaky voice.

Ima looked toward the door. So did Abba.

Then both their mouths opened in shock. No words came out.

In the doorway was a lamb. Hanging around her neck was a ribbon, as if she were a welcome home present, and her voice sounded a bit stuffy when she bleated, "meh-meh-meh."

The parents looked at each other, and for what was likely the first time in their lives, they were speechless.

~~~

"No, no, no," Ima finally said after a few, long moments. "A lamb is not going to live in the same house as me!"

"But Ima," Lali wailed, "please! Let's try it for just a week, then we'll see. If you don't agree, then next week, we'll send it to the petting zoo."

Ima stared at the lamb, and it seemed to be staring back at her.

"Meh?"

"Don't make me feel so bad about this," she told the lamb.

Then the fuzzy lamb came up to Ima and rubbed against her.

"Look! She likes you!" Lali announced joyfully.

Ima looked at the lamb. And the lamb let out another gentle "Mehhhhhh."

"Well, okay," Ima sighed, as she realized this was a losing battle. "But just for one week. And the minute this lamb gets out of control, she's going to be taken right back where she came from!"

"Oh, Ima!" Lali hugged her mother with all her heart.

"This was it. This was my biggest dream! Thank you!"

Lali could barely do anything else the rest of the day; she was just too excited. Her heart was overflowing with happiness, and she wanted her sisters to enjoy that level of happiness, too. How could she help make her sisters' dreams come true, just like Ima had made her dream come true? An opportunity arose very quickly.

## Chapter 17

# What Happened to Ayala?

Life flowed smoothly for the lamb in the Schneider household. At first. Ima couldn't believe that this was happening to her, but it was happening: there was a petting zoo in her home. Fortunately for Ima, Lali didn't ask to also bring the dusky grouper along (honestly, she wasn't sure that's what it was anymore, and she was afraid that Yoni would make fun of her, so she left it at Aunt Chana's house. That fish was back home in the sea the same day.)

On the roof of her house, the doves cooed, the lamb bleated, and there were a variety of flies, ants, worms, and other insects that joined the animal festival up there. Lali kept her word, and took care of the lamb all by herself. She fed it and gave it water, made sure it was clean and cared for, and also made sure the lamb wouldn't cause any trouble. Because she was small, the lamb could still be raised in a home setting.

"One week," Ayala announced to Lali when she came back from the grocery store one morning.

"What do you mean?" Lali asked.

"One week. You said a week. The lamb would live in our house for one week and then she'd go live in a nice petting zoo."

Lali paled. "That's right, I said that, but I said it would be a one-week trial, to see if she's bothering anyone, and—"

"And she's bothering someone!" Ayala declared.

"Who?"

"Me!"

"Why?"

"She bleats at night, and she's annoying in the morning, and she attracts flies at all hours of the day."

"There are no flies!" Lali defended her lamb. "Did you see one fly here because of her?"

"Did you expect the fly to come wearing a sign that says

'I came because of the lamb'? Flies come when there are animals."

"So why didn't you say that when Yoni was raising his pigeons?"

"Because there were no flies, and now there are."

Lali bristled. "You're just being mean to my lamb. She's clean and there isn't a single fly on her!"

"Well, fine." Ayala sighed. Since Chevy had left the house, she was rather lonely. Nechamy was very different from her, and she was much more forgiving of the kids' ideas and antics. Ayala had no ally. She fell silent, and Lali saw the silence as a way out. She quickly got herself ready for school and left. She noticed that something about Ayala's expression was odd. In the corner of her mind she made herself a note: try to figure out what was going on with her older sister.

Throughout that morning she didn't have a chance to speak to her sisters, so she announced an important meeting in her room after lunch, at three thirty.

"I think," Lali said when she convened her sisters for a strategy session, "that Ayala has been a bit sad recently."

"Because of the lamb?" Shevi asked hopefully. Deep in

her heart, she was quite afraid of the little animal, and preferred to see her out of the house. She was too kind to say anything to Lali about getting rid of the wooly creature that had joined their household, but she did hope that someone else would make it happen.

"What does that have to do with anything?" Lali asked. "Who would be upset about such a wonderful lamb?"

Shevi didn't want to tell Lali that she herself was quite upset, and that she was not sleeping peacefully at night. She was afraid the lamb would get out of her pen on the roof, carefully walk down the stairs, and come lick her face with that wet, pink tongue.

"I think," Chani said with her quiet yet confident voice, "that it's because Chevy got married."

"What does that have to do with it?" It was Riki's turn to wonder. "A wedding is a happy thing, not a sad one."

"That's right," Chani said. "At a wedding there's lots of excitement and happiness, but there's also a bit of sadness." She didn't tell them that she'd heard Shuey's conversation with their sister on the day of the wedding. He had been surprised and very bewildered when he saw Ima and his sisters shedding tears. He'd come to ask Ayala for an explanation.

*"Why did you cry?"*

*"Nechamy and Chani also cried a bit, and even Miri shed a few tears…" Ayala told him, as she stroked his cheek. "It's because we're very excited and emotional."*

*"Aren't you happy that she's getting married?" Shuey wanted to know.*

*"Of course we are! Ima's also very happy, but still…she also cried."*

*"Why?"*

*"First of all, because we are davening that Chevy should have a good life, that she should have children who are tzaddikim, and that they should have a home that is happy and full of Torah and yiras Shamayim. But in addition to all that, I do feel a bit bad, just a bit… After all, Chevy is the sister closest to me. We shared a room and we shared everything: stories, jokes, sad times, and happy things. And now she's leaving…"*

*"But she'll come visit!"*

*"Right, but it won't be the way it used to be. Tonight, I'll go home to our room and she won't be there…It's happy, but it's also a little sad…"*

Chani had heard that conversation, and it stuck in her mind. True, she had also shed tears, but they were tears of excitement. She didn't feel as close to their older sister as Ayala did. She felt closer to Nechamy and Miri, who were closer to her age. And Chani was finding it difficult to even imagine the day when each of them would move on to their own homes. *Maybe when that day comes*, she wondered, *you're big enough to handle the separation?*

"Do you understand?" she explained to her sisters. "This year, Binyamin moved to a different yeshivah, and now he doesn't come home at night. Chevy got married and doesn't live here anymore. Ayala is feeling lonely."

"We have to help her!" Lali declared.

## Chapter 18

### The Plan

"I cannot imagine," Riki said, "what we, girls aged nine and eleven, and even twelve, thirteen, and fourteen, can do to help someone who is eighteen."

"We can make her happy," Miri said thoughtfully.

"How? What do you think, that she's a little girl? That if we buy her a prize she'll be happy?"

"Oh, no," Etty said, remembering the story of the present for Kobi the driver. "I'm done with buying gifts for big adults who want a car!"

"Fine, I didn't mean that type of gift," Lali snapped. "And besides, if you had understood what the notes said in the first place, you wouldn't have messed up the whole thing so badly."

"Really?!" Etty was even more annoyed than Lali now. "And is it our fault that we got these garbled, faded, messy, confused notes? You should say thank you!"

When she noticed the threatening look on Etty's face, she changed her tone, and also the subject. "Umm. Thank you. Really. But we do have to think about something, because we can't allow someone to walk around our house looking so sad."

"Maybe she'd be happy if the lamb goes to the petting zoo?" Shevi suggested hopefully. "After all, you said yourself that she complained about the lamb."

"That's not what will make her happy," Lali said quickly. "The complaint was only...only...a tiny part of the problem. Something really minor...that doesn't even count."

Shevi was quiet. Her kind heart didn't let her ruin her younger sister's enthusiasm.

The girls sat and mulled over ideas. How could they, young girls without experience, cheer up their older sister? They weren't in high school so they weren't at the same school as she was, and they didn't know exactly how her days went. In fact, all they heard from her about school was the planning for overnights and for the school

Shabbaton — to the point that they wondered if girls in high school did anything else but plan events. Beyond that, they didn't know much.

"Maybe we should save up some money and send her on a fun trip?" Etty suggested. Since the trips they had taken with the London Schneiders, she was yearning for another one.

"Maybe we should buy her a book that she likes?" Miri suggested. Miri loved to read.

"Maybe each one of us could write her a letter of appreciation?" Chani offered — and of course, we know Chani loves to write.

"Perhaps we should hide a nosh she loves in her bag — or a different nosh each day?" Riki was suddenly enthused. "She'll be so busy trying to figure out who sent her the nosh and in the end we'll tell her that it was us!"

The girls exchanged glances. Of all the suggestions, that was the best one. It wasn't a one-time gift, with a short happy moment that would soon be over. It was something more complex. It was a long, ongoing gift, and there was also an element of mystery involved. Ayala would invest effort in solving the mystery, and she'd be distracted from this mild sadness that seemed to be surrounding her.

"That a pretty good idea," Chani said slowly. "We'll need to plan it out slowly, and make sure there are no holes in it."

"Holes in an idea?" Lali asked. "How could there be? An idea is not like a pair of tights!" She remembered her mother sighing, "There isn't a single pair of tights that lasts more than one wearing for you, Lali! It immediately grows holes!"

"Holes don't grow," Lali had explained innocently. "They just get holey for all kinds of reasons." She knew the reasons, but didn't offer details, because they weren't so nice to say: climbing on fences, picking withered leaves off a high tree, and all kinds of things like that. The same reasons that caused Tully's pants to look like a colander.

"There could be holes in an idea, if the idea is not a complete one," Chani explained to her younger sister. "Then the entire plan falls apart. If, let's say, someone is planning to travel to Haifa in order to be at a certain store at four o'clock, and he forgot that there is no bus that will get him to Haifa at four, and the bus will only get there at nine, when the store closes, then there was a hole in the idea. That means he forgot to think about one detail, and the whole plan is kaput."

"I see." Lali understood. "So we need to think about a whole idea, without holes. So that it will be successful."

"Exactly." Chani enjoyed her sister's quick grasp. "We need to see who can get it all arranged, without Ayala realizing that it's us, and without us nosing around in her stuff, which she doesn't like. We have to find exactly the things she likes to eat, and all kinds of details like that."

"Let's start," Lali said, looking important. "Let's get a pad, and we'll write down all the holes."

"No, just the opposite, we'll write down everything so it won't have holes," Miri said wisely. "Who has a pad?"

"I do." Etty, an avid collector of anything and everything, hurried to her room. She came back with a pink pad. "Here, I once got this from my *madrichah*. I have six or eight more like it."

"Who will write the details of the plan down on this pad?" Riki asked an important question.

Miri was chosen by a majority, because of her nice handwriting.

She opened the notebook and wrote a heading:

Operation Ayala

"No, what a name!" Riki grimaced. "Operation Simchah."

"Operation Nosh."

"Operation *V'ahavta Lereiacha.*"

"Operation What You Don't Like. Oh, as in 'don't do to a friend, what you don't like done to you,' which is the explanation of the mitzvah of *v'ahavta l'reiacha kamocha.*"

"What does that have to do with anything? We're doing just the opposite — we're making her happy."

"Operation *Vesamachta es rei'acha.*"

"There's no such *pasuk.*"

"So what? Is there a *pasuk* — Operation Ayala??"

"*Vesmachata bechol hatov* is a *pasuk.*"

"But it doesn't fit in here, because if she's happy with all the good there's no need to cheer her up."

"Actually, it makes sense, because after all the good we give her, she'll be happy."

And with that, "Operation *Vesamachata Bechol Hatov*" got underway.

 Chapter 19

## Vesamachta Bechol Hatov

"First we need to write down what she doesn't like," Riki said.

"It's better to write the things she *does* like."

"I don't mean nosh," Riki said solemnly. "I meant privacy. Ayala doesn't like it when people touch her stuff. She does let us touch her schoolbag, and she sometimes tells us, 'Bring my notebook from my bag,' or 'bring me a pen from the top drawer.' So these two things she lets us touch."

"Yes, because the rest of the drawers are very secret," Etty agreed. She'd once opened — by mistake — one of the drawers, and had been given a real dressing down by her normally calm sister. "And that's why we shouldn't ever open them."

"So the goal is to get the treats into her bag or the top drawer." Miri wrote:

*Goal: school bag or top drawer in the room.*

"What should we put in?"

"When?"

"Who should do it?"

"She likes chocolate, in every shape and type," Shevi said. She always noticed what her sisters liked. "And Bissli onion rings and Mexican nacho-flavor potato chips. Now let's count our money and see how much nosh it's enough for."

The meeting dispersed and each one of the girls went to check how much of a fortune she had. The loot was rather meager, taking into account that they had just bought some *afikoman* presents, birthday presents, and other treats.

"Should we include the boys?" Miri asked, but really, it was a statement.

"No!" Shevi and Riki declared.

"Why not?!" Miri was both surprised and a bit offended on behalf of her twin brother.

"Because they won't understand and they'll run to tell Ayala, and Ima, and everyone else about every little detail."

"I didn't mean the little boys," Miri said. "But Motty and Yoni?! They won't say anything. And Yoni has lots of money," she added slyly.

"Oh, okay," Riki grumbled. "But it's your responsibility if they ruin something."

"My responsibility," Miri agreed, fully trusting her twin brother. The girls finished the list and decided as follows: On Sunday, a bag of Mexican nacho-flavored potato chips would be stashed in Ayala's schoolbag, without any message.

On Monday they would put a strawberry-filled chocolate bar in the drawer, with a one-word note: "Enjoy!"

On Tuesday it would be the schoolbag's turn again, and they would put in a package of chocolate-covered cornflakes, with a two-word note: "With love."

On Wednesday, there would be Bissli onion rings in the drawer with a note: "All the best."

On Thursday, the Rosemarie chocolate in the schoolbag would have a four-word note: Have a sweet day!

On Friday, a fancy, parve Swiss chocolate bar would go on the desk with a note that said: Welcome to the Shabbos Queen. From all of us.

They reviewed their plan, and were very pleased indeed. The suspense grew with each word, and the final word — "us" — would make it clear to Ayala who was behind the mysterious gifts. The plan looked perfect. All that remained was to figure out how much Operation *Vesamachta Bechol Hatov* was going to cost. Riki and Etty, the usual shoppers, went to do some price checks. The rest of the girls sat down to rest and rejoice.

"Everything is so expensive," Etty said as she studied the stickers on the items they wanted to buy. "Where will we get so much money from? I barely have ten shekels."

"Let's write down how much each thing costs," Riki said practically. "We'll see how much money we're missing afterward."

They walked around the store and wrote down the prices. Then they left the store feeling like spies who had done a day's work in dangerous enemy territory. After doing the math, they saw that they had to get hold of forty shekels, and all they had was twenty-five.

"We could settle for cheaper nosh," Riki told Etty on their way home. "But you know, I like to give my sisters only the best."

"We'll have the boys join in. I'm sure they each have five or ten shekels for this very important cause."

"Let's hope," Riki said — and then almost collided headlong into Yoni, who was coming home from cheder. He was deep in thought and his head was down, chin nearly on his chest.

"Ahhh!!" The boy leaped away in fright and stared accusingly at the girls. "You!"

"Yes, us," Riki said. "Look where you're going."

"If I don't see, at least you should be looking," Yoni grumbled.

Riki decided to ignore his unreasonable response, because she had a more important thing on her mind: "Do you have money?"

Yoni eyed them suspiciously. "What for?"

"For Ayala." And they briefly told him about Ayala's

conversation with Lali, the meeting, and their important conclusions.

"I do," Yoni said, thinking for a minute. A strange expression crossed his face. "But I have to collect it."

"Collect it from where?"

"From all kinds of places," he answered evasively. "Come, let's go home, and I'll look."

"Should we help you?" Riki asked generously.

"No need." He seemed to be hiding a secret.

"If you don't want help, then I won't give it," Etty said cheerfully. "The main thing is that you bring the money so that we can finish this important mission."

Yoni turned to his room, still looking very mysterious. Riki and Etty exchanged glances. "What could it be already?" Etty shrugged. "What's the big mystery about his money? Does he have it? Great. If he doesn't? Neither do I. So what?" Etty was quite the spendthrift. She spent on herself and for others. Money she got for gifts did not last more than a day or two in her wallet. She generously bought small gifts for her brothers, nosh for her sisters, and little treats for herself. There usually wasn't more than a shekel or two left in her wallet.

"Good, I hope he brings something," Riki concluded. Honestly, she was very curious, and after a short silence, she admitted, "But I'm still wondering what his story is all about."

Chapter 20

## The Bag of Money

Yoni went over to his drawer and rummaged around inside it. Gloomily, he began to collect the coins. There were mostly ten *agorot* coins, a few half-shekel coins, and very few whole shekels. Now, you try to collect fifty-two shekels from a drawer in ten *agorot* coins!

How had Yoni gotten into this embarrassing situation? Why had he exchanged his money, which had been very nicely stored mostly as two twenty-shekel bills, into a silly batch of coins?

This is what happened:

In Yoni's class, an announcement was made that they would be buying a gift for the afternoon *rebbi*. Why? Because he was leaving and a new *rebbi* would be taking his place.

"Who will volunteer to collect the money?" Shimshi asked loudly, expecting the regular volunteers — Shloimy or Dovid — to offer.

Yoni's voice surprised him. "Me!"

"Really?!" Shimshi turned around and studied him with surprise. "You??"

Yoni's confidence wavered a bit when he saw Shimshi's disbelief. "Yes, me," he repeated. "Aren't I good for the job?"

"Why not? Yes, yes, you're very good," Shimshi answered. But his eyes sent another message altogether. It was clear to everyone that he thought Yoni was not suited for the job at all. And why had Yoni offered to volunteer for this? Because for a long time, his mother's words about his behavior in class — and behavior with other people in general — had been echoing in his mind.

"I'm very happy that you are such a big *talmid chacham* and *masmid*, Yoni," she said to him. "But you also have to learn how to live with your friends. It's so important. You can't completely cut off from the other boys. You have to be more…social. Talk to the boys, laugh at their jokes, chat about silly things. You're still a kid! You need this." Ima had told him these words more than just once or twice, and he had kept her words in mind. Now he had an opportunity to interact with other boys besides Dovi, who he was already a bit friendly with.

"Fine," replied Shimshi. Unlike Yoni, whose confidence was now shaken, Shimshi quickly regained his own footing. He gave the job of treasurer over to his classmate. "Here is the list of names of the boys, and here you make a checkmark next to whoever brought, and then put the money in a bag. It's very easy. If you want help buying the gift, I'm willing to come with you."

Yoni, confused and hesitant, nodded. What could be simpler than making a check next the name of every boy who brought money?! It was so simple...but now he needed to talk to all his friends and to remind them, nudge them, plead with them. He was so put off by conversation with other boys, and all the talking...but he had no choice. He couldn't back down now.

"You each need to bring the money. Two shekels," Shimshi announced loudly. "And give it to Yoni, because he's doing the collecting."

So, from now he was the treasurer. It was a job suited for a boy in the center of the action, someone more popular...and that was so not who he was.

"Do you want help?" Dovi suddenly appeared next to him just at the minute he needed him.

"Oh, Dovi, good thing you came," he said with relief. "I just…volunteered…I don't know why."

"What did you volunteer for?" Dovi asked curiously.

"To collect money. Is it very hard?" he asked hesitantly.

"You have to chase everyone to bring it," Dovi said, from past experience. "But it's not very complicated. You just have to remind everyone every day."

So simple. Remind. Everyone. Every day! Yoni sighed. How had he gotten into this? He almost went to Shimshi to say that in the end he wouldn't be able to do it. But he was too embarrassed. Shimshi had been doing this for years, and sometimes Dovi or Dovid took over from him. Ruvi or Shloimy also collected money at different times. Couldn't he give some of his time and energy even once? He could, and he would.

So the nudging began.

Yoni noted with satisfaction that he was feeling a bit closer and more connected to the other boys in the class. There wasn't a single boy he didn't approach to ask when he would be bringing the money. A lot of the boys gave right away, but some of them needed to be reminded over and over. Shimshi helped him, and so did Dovi, who accompanied Yoni like a loyal shadow throughout all the nudging and reminding and urging. Anyone who had ever collected money for gifts at the end of the year or for Purim, or any other event, could identify with Yoni's joy when his bag was filled with fifty-two shekels — most of them in ten *agorot* coins.

"Now," Yoni said with satisfaction to Dovi, "we need to go buy the gift."

"Should I come with you?"

"Sure." Yoni didn't know what and how to choose.

"Good. We'll buy him a *sefer*. I'm sure he needs one. Let's go!"

Yoni asked permission from Ima and then took the stairs two at a time. His heart was pounding with excitement after he had invested so much effort into this project. He had taken on a very social job, and had succeeded!

Dovi walked next to him, less excited and a lot more practical than Yoni. They chatted about the test next week and about how the winning class would get a special trip!

"You are in our class, so we're sure to win, the question is where the trip will be to," Dovi said.

"I think," Yoni began excitedly, waving the bag with the money, "that we should go to —"

Yoni hadn't noticed the nail sticking out of a tree they were walking past. The bag got caught on the nail…and the whole side tore open.

Stunned at the scene, the boys just gaped at hundreds of coins scattering every which way. The coins seemed thrilled at their freedom, and escaped and hid, rolled and scattered, and — left the bag completely empty….

## Chapter 21

### *Runaway Coins*

Dovi began to chase the coins.

The coins themselves were thrilled to be free, and fled as if they had feet.

In a second, they spun like dreidels, flew like butterflies, escaped like ants scurrying out of the rain, and twirled like grain husks in the wind.

Yoni himself was so stunned he could not move.

"Why are you standing like that?" Dovi chided his friend. "Let's pick up the money!" He ran to and fro like a bulldozer on a building site, his fingers scrabbling for every shiny object. "See how I'm bending down — you should also do something!"

As he spoke, he picked up what looked like a coin,

but turned out, in the glow of the streetlight, to be a withered leaf. Dovi felt a tickle on his finger and threw the leaf back down in disgust. "Ugh! What was that?"

An ant remained on his finger, seeming to glare at him in rebuke. "Ahhh! Yoni!! Look!"

The ant paced back and forth on his finger, and she seemed to be rather enjoying her new perch. "Ooooh! Yoni, help me!"

Yoni, still in shock, and very unmoved by Dovi's screaming, blew on the ant, which flew off Dovi's finger. He wondered what Dovi would say about Lali's ant collection. The thought was funny, but he didn't even feel the urge to smile. This situation was not funny at all. Here he was, standing frozen in place, in the evening darkness, with coins scattered all around him…and he had to find them and make sure he had a whole fifty-two shekels! He needed to rummage through ant nests, dig holes in the sand, and grope blindly after hundreds of coins! Maybe even thousands! Yoni's brilliant mind was already calculating: if all the boys had paid him with ten *agorot* coins, then he would have needed to find five hundred and twenty coins! He felt dizzy, and almost fell over. It was a good thing that Dovi grabbed his shirt collar and exclaimed: "Help me! Why are you standing there like a wooden pole?!"

Yoni immediately sank to the ground. "Is this better?" he asked sadly.

"Why did you sit down?!" Dovi was even more annoyed now.

"You asked why I'm standing like a wooden pole, so I figured you don't want to me to be standing!"

"I didn't mean you should *sit down*! I meant that you should help me!"

"Oh." Yoni pretended not to have understood, and reached out and fingered a few coins. "I don't even know how many half shekels and how many ten *agorot* coins there were!"

The darkness was growing heavier, because the sun had set and the nearest streetlight was a good few feet away. Dovi looked at Yoni with despair. "What should we do?"

"How much did you pick up already?"

Dovi had a few dozen coins that he had wrapped into a tissue. A quick count showed that he had five shekels and twenty *agorot*. He let out a long, frustrated sigh. "After hours of work, this is what I got?!"

"Don't overdo it, it hasn't been hours, just a few minutes," Yoni said, rummaging in his pocket for a bag that would be better than the tissue. His efforts came just in time, because at that moment, they heard a rustle, a tearing noise, and the poor tissue gave out — and tore to shreds. Dovi stared in disbelief at how all his efforts were now scattered once again in the sand.

"Whoa!! What chutzpah of this tissue!" Dovi fumed. "Did you see what it did?"

"Don't blame it. Tissues aren't meant to carry heavy coins," Yoni defended the tissue, which was now lying in pieces on the ground. "Look, I found the bag from my sandwich. That'll work. Let's collect the coins."

The two friends bent over the sandy ground, feeling around for lost coins. Every so often, Dovi gave a strangled cry when his fingers touched an ant or a ladybug. Yoni laughed at him at first, but when he smashed a poor worm between his fingers, he stopped laughing.

"We need to be careful," he said with a serious expression, "not to do *tza'ar baalei chaim.*"

"Right. But when I was trying not to mush all those ants you didn't say that," Dovi pointed out.

Yoni did not reply. They stacked the coins into a pretty big pile and began to count. They were disappointed to learn that they had collected only ten shekels and thirty *agorot.* "I'm going." Dovi quickly jumped up.

"Where to?" Yoni leaped up and stood in front of his friend. "Don't leave me here alone!"

"I'm going to get a flashlight. We can't work like this. You stay to guard the money, so that no one takes it."

"There's no chance someone will want to take it," Yoni grumbled. "Spending an hour collecting money only to find out that you have five shekels? Soon enough it will be dawn, and then we'll find the money easily."

"Don't worry. I'm going, and I'll be right back," Dovi promised. He began to run toward his house. Yoni pinned a lot of hopes on the flashlight to help them see what was a coin and what was a leaf. He was tired of leaves, pebbles, bugs, and pieces of paper that turned out to be everything except a ten-*agorot* or half-shekel coin. He put his hand in his pocket to see if he had a tissue to wipe the sweat off his forehead, and he discovered a treasure: the stub of a candle that he had stuck in his pocket after one of his experiments, and a package of matches! What a find!

He carefully lit the candle and put it on the floor next to him. That's how Dovi found him, like a real *talmid chacham* sitting and learning by the light of the candle. But Yoni wasn't learning, he was searching for missing coins by the flickering flame….

## Chapter 22

## The Secret of the Coins

The flashlight's beam was thin and dim. Yoni claimed the candle was stronger than Dovi's flashlight. Dovi didn't argue, especially since he realized that the battery of the flashlight was fading. Yoni's candle was more reliable.

The two groped around in the light of the candle, crawling on all fours and touching every grain of sandy soil, every piece of paper; they cleaned the area from taffy wrappers, advertisements, pieces of paper of all kinds, and yes, little insects. But the stubborn coins kept hiding. Some of them emerged from the ground after desperate digging and others remained in the ground as if this was their rightful place since the world began.

"Enough! That's it!" Dovi got up, and straightened his

aching back. "And I don't care how many coins are left here!"

Yoni also got up, and brushed off his pants from the sand. "Neither do I!" he declared. But he did care. They sat down on the nearest bench and counted the money. Thirty-six shekels and seventy *agorot*.

"Not bad, considering how hard this was," Yoni reflected.

"But not great, after all that effort," Dovi objected.

"The stores are closing soon. I'll keep the coins and pay with my own money. Then tomorrow we'll come back and keep searching," Yoni decided. Dovi agreed. Halfheartedly, they went to the nearest *seforim* store, and Yoni wondered again and again how it could be that all the strange stories always happened to him.

After the goodbye party and the giving of the gift, Dovi gave a speech to the *rebbi* and his friends about the importance of small details. None of his friends knew why he was exchanging glances with Yoni.

The two agreed to meet again at recess between the morning and afternoon lessons, near the tree. In daylight, they hoped it would be easier to find some of the lost coins.

Indeed, the shining sun didn't just light up the whole area, it also reflected off the coins and made them twinkle in the sun. Now the boys found it much easier to work, and they soon found another twelve shekels and sixty *agorot*. They were missing less than three shekels.

"Maybe a poor person will find it and will buy some bread to revive himself," Dovi said poetically.

"I don't think a poor person will find my money, and if he does, I don't think that with less than three shekels he can buy a loaf of bread to revive himself. It's barely enough for one roll."

"I didn't say he should buy a loaf, he should buy one meal's worth," Dovi explained.

"No one buys such an amount today. In the past, you could buy half a loaf of bread. Today you can't do that either," Yoni said impatiently. "Come on already! I'm tired and hungry and I'm totally sick of this story with the coins!!"

And that was the reason why Yoni preferred to change the money before he gave it to Etty. His money was now made up of tens of *agorot*, and he was embarrassed to tell her how it had happened. If she heard the whole story, she wouldn't understand how it could have happened to him. She was always collecting money from her classmates for gifts, and nothing like this had ever happened to her. No, he preferred that his siblings not find out about the story. The one time he had mustered up the courage to collect money, and then this....

Yes, changing the money was the simplest solution. But how? He pondered for a minute, and then headed over to the tzedakah boxes in the house. Hopefully, he would be able to exchange tens of *agorot* for shekels, or even five-shekel coins. On his way down from his room to the dining room, the coins rattled loudly in his pocket. He was afraid the whole family would come to see what the racket was about. He was happy when he didn't meet anyone; only when he reached the tzedakah boxes, did he find Bentzy, swaying with *kavanah*.

"What do you want?" Bentzy grumbled. "Don't you see I'm davening?"

"What are you davening?"

"That Aunt Chana should have children," Bentzy shared

what was on his mind. "Because she's probably very sad that we left."

"I'm doubtful that she's sad that children who brought live fish, and took her boat without permission, and terrified her so much that she had to call the police, and then even brought a lamb, finally left," Yoni said scornfully. "She's probably happy that you left."

"*We* left! Not *you* left! *You* were also there."

"Yes, but I didn't do anything silly, like you did," Yoni said. "And besides, I think she's too old, and she can't have children."

"Ahhh," Bentzy sighed deeply. "But Sarah Imeinu was ninety and she had Yitzchak."

"That was a special miracle."

"And I'm davening for another special miracle." The boy looked very serious. "I also gave money to tzedakah for this."

"That's very nice of you," Yoni said with a smile. "Now, please go do a different mitzvah because I also need to do something important."

Bentzy scampered off and Yoni opened the tzedakah boxes in order to exchange his coins for larger ones in the boxes. He found five one-shekel coins, one five-shekel coin and one two-shekel coin. Pleased, he put his coins into the boxes. Once he was done, he went to find Etty so he could give her his contribution to the cause.

## Chapter 23

### Candy from Heaven

That day, Tully returned from cheder in a very grumpy mood. This was rather rare, because Tully was by nature very cheerful and kind. He had an easygoing personality. He was friends with most of the kids in his class, and his teachers liked him very much, even though he was quite mischievous and had big ideas. It was impossible not to like that active, cheerful little boy with the impossible ideas.

But still, that day, he was in a terrible mood. First of all, Yossi had fought with him. And Yossi was to blame. Tully had pointed out that it's not a good idea to play with marbles in the sand, because they could get lost. Yossi said he didn't care. After his prediction had come true, and Yossi had lost two marbles, he blamed Tully for the loss. What a chutzpah! And he had clearly told him not to play there!

That was the first thing.

Then his new ball had popped because of the thorny bush, and in the end, he'd lost his water bottle that Ima had prepared. So he was also very thirsty.

He stormed into the house. "Ima!!!"

"Yes?" she answered in her calm voice. "And hello to you, too, Tully."

"Oh, hello," Tully snapped. "It's all Yossi's fault…and I'm thirsty."

"Here, have a drink." Ima gave him a cold drink of water.

"I want soda!" he protested.

"We drink water. On Shabbos we have sweet drinks."

Tully drank, and wanted to tell Ima about the marbles and the ball. But first, he had to sweeten his day with something. "Fine. So I want a nosh."

"Here's a cookie and a wafer you can take," Ima said, and hurried over to Eli who had just fallen over and had started to cry.

"Ugh," Tully grumbled aloud. "No one cares about me in this house!" He said it quietly, because he knew it wasn't true. But he had to say it to calm himself down a bit.

Ayala heard him. "What are you talking about, cutie?" she protested aloud. "Come here, tell me what happened."

Tully shuffled over to his older sister. True, Ima was much better, but Ayala could also listen. He told her about the marbles and the ball and that Yossi was fighting with him and that he had been so hot. Ayala listened and sympathized, and he felt a bit better. Ayala knew how to listen and to empathize with him. Now he felt better.

"Can you please go get me my good pen?" she asked him, once he had calmed down. "It's in my briefcase, which is on the chair in my room."

Tully leaped up and ran to the second floor. It's true that he was a bit calmer but he still wanted a nosh. Badly. The cookie — well, what was a cookie worth? It wasn't even a good nosh! *I want potato chips*! he thought to himself. *And Mexican nachos if possible, that's the best one*!

He opened Ayala's schoolbag to get her pen, and froze. Inside Ayala's bag there was a bag of potato chips!!!

"Ayala!!!" he yelled.

"Yes?! Did you find it?!"

"Did you put a nosh for tomorrow in your bag?"

"Of course not!" she exclaimed. "I'm on a diet!"

Diet. His sisters were always on a diet. So strange. Who wanted to be on a diet and not eat anything yummy?! That made no sense at all.

Whatever it was, he quickly moved on. Ayala's diet was not important now. What *was* important was the potato chips! It wasn't hers! But it was in her bag... maybe Hashem had sent him the potato chips because he had davened for them? Then they were certainly not Ayala's....

Well, he'd keep the chips in his drawer for now, and he would try to figure out who they belonged to.

The next day, Tully waited for a good time. He hovered around Ayala, who was studying for a test in the dining room, like a bee over a pot of honey.

"What do you want, little kiddo?" Ayala laughed, when she saw her little brother going in circles around her.

"I'm not little!" he was miffed. "Tell me, do you want me to bring you something from your room?"

"Why?" Ayala looked at him suspiciously. "Don't go painting it black or anything!"

"Of course not!" Tully was offended for the second time, and put on his most innocent looking face. "Me?! How could I do such a terrible thing?!"

"Simple, not long ago, you did just such a terrible thing." Ayala laughed. "But if you want, I really need my old grammar notebook, the one with the pink doodles on it. It's in my drawer."

"I'll go get it!" Tully leaped up like he'd been shot out of a cannon. "I'm going right now!"

"Do you have a contest about helping your brothers and sisters or something?" Ayala called after him.

"No, I'm just a good boy who always wants to help!" he answered back.

Before opening the drawer, he said in a trembling voice: "Hashem, please, I want yummy chocolate. It doesn't matter which one."

He opened the drawer. He closed his eyes. And opened them again. His face paled in shock. Someone had put strawberry-filled chocolate in the drawer. He touched it with trembling fingers. This was too strange to be true. A real mystery, that someone experienced in solving mysteries (like him!) would just have to solve.

## Chapter 24

### The Mystery

"You won't believe it," Tully told Bentzy almost shaking with excitement. "It's a mystery that we have to solve!" At first, he had planned to keep the whole mystery to himself. "I'm not telling anyone anything," he repeated to himself all the way back to the dining room. "I'm not telling anyone anything," he said in a quiet voice that grew stronger. "Nothing to anyone. Anything to no one. Nothing. Zero. To anyone. Not telling. No one anything."

"Did you bring the notebook?" Ayala heard her brother muttering strangely, but she'd known him long enough to know that he could be so engrossed in his active imagination that he could even forget that he was at home. He could be imagining that he was in a space ship and the people around him were astronauts, like him. If Etty would talk to him, for example, he'd look at her in surprise. How had she gotten into his spaceship?

"Notebook?" Tully shook off his dreams and his mysteries. "Which notebook?"

"You went up to my room to bring me a notebook because you're a good boy who likes to help." Ayala laughed.

"Oh, yes, right." And he raced back to the room to find the notebook, and brought it to his sister. "The pilot is landing!" he announced. "With the goods that he got!"

He handed Ayala the notebook and ran back to his room. The whole way he kept practicing the important words. "So what if it's very interesting? I'm not telling it to anyone. That's it. Final. No one. I'm not telling anyone about this mystery. It's my mystery and I don't want anyone else to mix in. Not telling anyone anything! Not Sruly, not Shuey, not Bentzy, no one! It's my secret! I'm not saying!"

He went into his room and found Bentzy, who was busy making a truck out of Lego.

"I'm not telling you," Tully said right when he walked in. "And don't ask me, because it's final!"

"What are you not telling?" Bentzy was hardly interested. His eyes were focused on the truck's wheels. How could it be that he wasn't able to put them on? There was a piece jutting out here that was bothering him....

"That there's a mystery that needs to be solved!"

"A mystery?" Bentzy looked up, as a spark of curiosity spread in his eyes. "Which mystery? Like the light in the staircase?"

"No, no." Both of them, and Shuey, were still sore and insulted that their brothers had not shared the mystery with them then, before Chevy's engagement. "Something much more...dramatic!" (He'd learned the word from Yoni and he liked using it.)

"What?" Bentzy was getting more curious.

"But I'm not telling anyone. Not even you."

"Really? You won't tell *me*?" Bentzy was disappointed. Tully was already regretting that he'd said he wouldn't share. Bentzy *had* to know. If not, who would help him? This was a mystery straight from mystery land, and they would need to do serious surveillance, like real detectives.

"You won't believe it," he said excitedly. "It's a mystery that we have to solve!"

"Fine, fine," Bentzy said. "Just tell me what it is already!"

"I found nosh!"

"Is that all?" Bentzy turned back to his car, disappointed. "I also found nosh once. In Ima's cabinet."

"No, no," Tully tried to explain. "I wanted a nosh, and then I found it!"

"The nosh?"

"Yes! In Ayala's drawer!"

Bentzy was puzzled. "You went to Ayala's drawer and there you found nosh that you wanted."

"Yes!"

"How could that be?"

"It must be a miracle," Tully said, still shaking. "But maybe it's only a mystery and not a miracle. So we have to check it out!"

Bentzy agreed that it was worth checking out. "Why did you go to Ayala's drawer in the first place?"

"Because she wanted me to."

"So maybe she hid something there for you?"

"She didn't. I asked her if she put a nosh in her bag and she said she's on a diet. So I realized it's not her, and the nosh got there by itself."

"It didn't get there by itself. Nosh doesn't have legs," Bentzy said scornfully. "Maybe someone heard you say that you want a nosh and hid it in her drawer for you?"

"At first it was in her schoolbag. But it doesn't matter. If someone wants to hide a nosh for me, why put it in Ayala's bag?!"

Bentzy couldn't argue with that logic.

"Fine," Bentzy said as he tried to shrug off the grandness of the mystery. "So let's go and ask everyone who put it there and why. Someone put it in her bag. That's for sure." Tully was insulted and horrified at the same time. "Is that why I shared this with you??" he gasped. "I want a mystery, with suspects and wild chases, and evidence, and you're ruining it all?! Slow down! First off, we need to write down a list of suspects, then decide who is going to watch people, and only in the end do an investigation!"

Bentzy agreed. Because, after all, if they went right away and asked everyone, then they would discover the answer to the mystery too quickly and easily. And they really wanted to have a tough mystery to solve!

"Do you think she didn't notice?" Etty asked Miri.

"Why? Because she's not saying anything?" Miri replied.

They were on the way to school on the third day of their operation. Miri looked in her little pad and saw that today they were supposed to put a a bag of chocolate-covered cornflakes in Ayala's bag, with a note that said "With Love."

"Yes! We're making an effort and she doesn't even care!" Etty argued heatedly. "We collected money, thought a lot about it, and she doesn't even look suspicious or happy or surprised!"

"Let's wait another day," Chani said firmly. "Maybe she didn't realize yet that it's from us."

"Could be. But why isn't she saying anything? Asking something?!"

They didn't know that Ayala hadn't seen even one of the treats. Both things that they had hidden in her bag and in her drawer were resting securely in Tully's drawer, waiting for the mystery to be solved.

## Chapter 25

### *Who Dunnit?*

We don't have a list of suspects," Bentzy said. "The whole family are suspects."

"That means we do have suspects — twenty-one suspects!" Tully protested.

"Tzivi, Tammy, and Eli are not suspects and neither is Gila," Bentzy claimed. "They're too little."

"Fine, and there are also all Ayala's friends," Tully sighed. "How can we do such a hard investigation?"

"Let's forget the list of suspects," Bentzy suggested. "We'll just do stakeouts."

"Stake-whats?"

"It means we'll follow the suspects."

"But if we don't have a list of suspects, how can we follow them?"

"Umm…. So we'll follow….um…we'll stake out the crime scene!" Bentzy shouted.

"Crime scene?" Tully asked. "What's that?"

"Yoni told me about it. It's what you call the place where the crime took place. A crime is a bad thing."

"Crime? Putting in nosh is the opposite of a crime!" Tully protested. "I want everyone to do crimes like this."

"You don't understand! It became a crime scene because we're investigating it. Besides, who said they had permission?"

"Fine. So we're going to stake out Ayala's room?" Tully didn't sound excited. "It's very boring. I thought detectives do more interesting stuff than stand around staring at a boring room for lots of hours."

"They have to do stuff like that. Otherwise, they won't see who's coming."

"From tomorrow." Tully pushed off the operation. "Tomorrow we'll start the crime scene thing."

During school, Miri pondered Etty's words. She was right. They were putting this nosh in their sister's bag and drawer, and she wasn't reacting at all. She didn't ask, she didn't tell Ima that something was going on, nothing. That was very strange indeed!

Miri studied her list.

*On the first day: the schoolbag. The treat: Mexican nacho potato chips. Without a note.*

*On the second day: The drawer. The treat: Strawberry filled chocolate with a one-word note: Enjoy!*

*On the third day: The schoolbag again. The treat: chocolate-covered cornflakes with two words: With love.*

*The fourth day: The drawer. The treat: Onion Rings Bissli with three words: All the best.*

*The fifth day: The bag. The treat: Rosemarie chocolate with a four-word message: Have a sweet day!*

*The sixth day: On the desk. The treat: Bittersweet chocolate with the note: Welcome to the Shabbos Queen, from all of us.*

It was such a great plan, but Ayala, for some reason was not cooperating. She didn't ask or try to figure out what was going on. And she wasn't talking about it. At all.

Miri put her pen down and thought hard. Could it be that Ayala's situation was so serious that she wasn't even taking an interest in her surroundings? That didn't seem to be the case. So who could give her advice about their failed plan?

She made a decision: If, by tomorrow, Ayala did not react at all, she'd tell Ima the secret. It's true, they wanted to keep it a secret, but maybe Ayala needed more help than just a treat?!

Maybe there was something really serious going on.

"Do you want me to bring you something from your room?" Tully asked Ayala, who was studying, as usual, in the dining room.

"What's the story with my room?" Ayala demanded to know. "What do you want from it?"

"Me? Nothing." Tully got a bit nervous. If Ayala would realize that her bag had become a source of nosh, she might take all his treasures away! And why did she need nosh anyway? She was on a diet!

"Every day you want to go into my room, for some secret reason, and I want to know the reason!" Ayala insisted.

"Fine, if you don't want me to bring you something from your room you don't need to." Tully looked as innocent as he could, as if he didn't know what anyone wanted from such an innocent, kind boy.

"I really do need a notebook and a book that I forgot in my room," Ayala said, a bit sheepishly. She liked studying in the big, quiet empty dining room, with the air conditioning on high and the doors closed. She usually forgot to take everything she needed with her, and often looked for volunteers to help. Her curiosity (to know what Tully was looking for in her room) and her laziness (not to go up to her room herself) were competing inside her, until the laziness won out: "Fine, go and bring it for me, okay?"

"I'm on my way!" the little tzaddik said as he began to run.

On the way to Ayala's room, Tully announced. "Now, look how amazing. I'm telling you that I want a nosh, and you'll see how Hashem sends it through Ayala's schoolbag."

Bentzy's eyes were sparkling. He was about to experience a miracle! Or at least something that very closely resembled a miracle. He would see how it all happened!

"Which nosh should I choose today?" Tully mused importantly. "Well, today I want either a candy or a taffy, something sweet."

He opened the bag and didn't see anything. Bentzy was ready and waiting to make fun of him, but then Tully quickly opened the drawer.

A little package of chocolate-covered cornflakes was resting there. Whole and perfect. Bentzy's eyes gleamed. "It's not a taffy," he said after a moment of awed silence. "Or a candy."

"Yes, but I said something sweet also, and chocolate is sweet," Tully defended his request. "Tell me it's not a miracle!"

"It is," Bentzy said, and began to think who could have done it. "But who could have put this chocolate here like this, and why?"

"For me, what do you mean?"

"I don't think all this nosh is for you," Bentzy said seriously.

"Why not??" Tully pouted.

"Because it's not your schoolbag or your drawer. It's Ayala's and that's why it's hers." Bentzy shared the logic behind his decision.

"But I'm the one who asked! She didn't even know about it! It's my request from Hashem!" Tully defended his nosh. "And she's on a diet!"

"It doesn't matter," Bentzy said sternly. "I think it's hers and you can even ask Abba if I'm right."

## Chapter 26

# *The End of the Nosh*

"So am I right?" Tully concluded his story and waited for his father's response. "Right if Hashem sent me this nosh I can eat it? Bentzy says I can't. I think I can, and not only because I really want the nosh! I think it's all mine! I asked Hashem and He gave it to me!"

Abba cleared his throat, and then again — and again.

"*Nu*, Abba," Tully said, looking wide-eyed at his father. "Say something!"

"I want to tell you a story," Abba said. "Call everyone and I'll tell the story."

Tully dashed out of the dining room, and screamed as loud as he could: "Story!! Abba!!! Wants!!! To tell!!!"

He didn't need more than that for doors to start

slamming and children to start running down the halls in search of a story. In a minute, the dining room was filled with sixteen children. Chevy wasn't there, of course, and neither were the two *bochurim*. Tzivi and Eli also weren't there. Tammy was carried in by Miri, who had been holding her.

Abba looked around at his children calmly and then said: "Let me tell you a story. The older ones might know it, but it's always good to hear it again.

"Many years ago, a poor, good-hearted man lived in Tzfas. He loved Hashem and feared Him. One day, this Jew heard from the *rav* about the *lechem hapanim* that was placed on the *Shulchan* in the Beis Hamikdash, and that the *kohanim* would replace it each week. Since the Beis Hamikdash was destroyed, this innocent man heard, the *lechem hapanim* is no longer. He was very distraught over this, and after discussing it with his wife, they decided to place nicely braided challos in the *aron kodesh* each week. This way, Hakadosh Baruch Hu would have bread, like He had in the time of the Beis Hamikdash. The poor *shamash* of the shul discovered this, and each Erev Shabbos, he took the challos and joyfully ate them over Shabbos. He thought this was a form of *matan b'seser*, secretly giving tzedakah. The well-meaning Jew was so pleased that Hashem took his bread, and he kept up this practice for many years. One day, the *rav* met him when he was placing the challos inside the *aron kodesh*, and rebuked him for thinking that Hashem took his offering. But that night, the Arizal came to the *rav* in a dream and said that since the day the Beis Hamikdash was destroyed, Hakadosh Baruch Hu had not had such *nachas ruach* like that which came about through this Yid's actions. Now that the *rav* had stopped it, he would be punished, and would pass away that year. And that's what happened."

Abba finished the story, and everyone's eyes were wide open with expectation. Only Tully, who had raised the whole issue, did not understand.

"*Nu?*" he asked Abba impatiently. "I didn't understand. Am I allowed to take the nosh or not?"

"You don't understand?" Sruly's eyes sparkled. "You're like the *shamash* — you told Hashem to send you the nosh and you got it, and since then, the bond between you and Hashem got stronger!"

Tully mulled this over for a minute. "I asked and He sent it to me," he repeated Sruly's words. "But now I hear that it wasn't even for me!"

"Maybe," Ayala said. "Maybe it is yours. In a special kind of way."

"So will you give me the nosh?" Tully asked hopefully.

"No way!" her sisters cut in. They had come up with the idea and contributed the money. They had been through so much to get that money!

"Forget about it!" Yoni added. He'd collected coins in the dark, accidently mashing bugs between his fingers in his quest for those precious ten *agorot* coins.

"I also want!" Shuey and Bentzy cried together.

"It's for you, so you should be happy!" Miri said.

"So you shouldn't feel so lonely," Chani elaborated.

"Because you're big already and it could be that you're not so interested in the younger ones anymore," Riki explained.

"Maybe soon you'll see that even though Chevy got married, we're also interesting!" Etty cried.

"And maybe my lamb annoys you a little...." Lali sounded apologetic.

Shevi just looked at her sister, and, having nothing to add, she remained quiet, in her shy way. Ayala's eyes seemed shiny. Her sisters looked at each other, puzzled. Was she crying again?

"Are you crying?" Tully sounded alarmed. "So forget it, you can keep the nosh! Here!" And one after another, he pulled out the treats he had been hoarding.

"You are such wonderful siblings," Ayala said. "And I'm not crying, Tully, I'm just touched that you thought of me, all of you." *In such a family*, she thought happily, *it's impossible to feel lonely even for a minute*!

While everyone was talking, little Gila decided to take some action. There was nosh in a nice pile on the table, and while her siblings were busy, she very quietly opened the packages. One after another. Chips. Chocolate. More chocolate.

"Gila!!!" Lali shrieked when she realized what was going on. The Schneider children and their father turned around to see the cause of her concern. They discovered Gila covered in chocolate, and glowing with pride, as she stuck her fingers into the crumbs that remained of the potato chips. In one hand she held the empty bag, and in the other, she held a dripping, melted chocolate bar. She was licking the oozing chocolate off her fingers with her little tongue.

"I guess it really wasn't my nosh," Ayala laughed.

"You ate it all?!" asked Tully. He and Bentzy couldn't believe how their treasure had gotten away.

"Not all!" she replied, waving a tiny piece of potato chip. "I didn't eat everything! This is for the lamb."

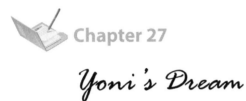

### Chapter 27

## *Yoni's Dream*

Much to her delight, now the whole story with the nosh — and how it was eaten up — had pushed aside the question of her lamb. Lali hoped it would stay that way — then maybe the lamb could stay! The one-week trial had already passed and Ima hadn't said a word as to whether Buma (the name she gave her) could stay. And that's why she was also keeping quiet.

The lamb, thought Lali, was behaving beautifully. For lambs, her behavior was truly impressive. She got up at dawn, which meant that Lali had to get up as well, before Buma's baa-baaing would wake up the family and the neighbors. Lately Lali thought that the lamb was suffering from a slight cold, because instead of saying "meh-meh," she was bleating "beh-beh." Lali was a bit worried, and almost wanted to ask a veterinarian, but Yoni waved off her worries. She hoped he was right.

Lali got up when the alarm clock rang — at dawn — and began to care for her lamb. She fed her, cleaned the pen, and took her out for a morning walk on the roof. *Baruch Hashem* they had done renovations and the roof had been expanded so much; this way there was room for Buma to walk around back and forth in the clear air. When Buma went to rest, Lali got ready for school, but not before she left her plenty of food, water, and fresh milk. She then locked the door to the roof so the little lamb wouldn't try to get out, and fall down the stairs.

After that Lali had to say goodbye to her lamb for the rest of the morning, when she sat in class and tried to figure out how to multiply a number by zero, only to discover that it had turned into zero itself.

Life with lammy went smoothly like this for many days. Two whole weeks passed with Buma living with the Schneiders and everyone had his or her own way of dealing with the lamb.

Ima didn't say a word. Ayala, after the generous outpouring of nosh and kindness, didn't say anything either. Lali secretly made a mental check next to Ayala's name. Her sister looked more cheerful, and her sad face was softened by smiles more often. Lali was happy about that. Her plan to cheer up her sister had worked! And indirectly, she had also helped her Buma stay in the house. Until when? She didn't know. Surely within a few months — or a few years, she'd need to ask Yoni — Buma would become an adult sheep, and then there was no doubt she'd have to go to a farm or a petting zoo. But for now, Lali was raising the lamb with all the love and warmth that she had in her.

One afternoon, Lali sat and stroked the little lamb's face, and the animal licked Lali's hand and every so often let out a bleat: "Beh!"

Suddenly Yoni dashed onto the roof in a hurry, toppling a few things on his way.

"Hello," Lali said calmly.

"What? Oh," he said distractedly as he walked over to his beloved pigeons; he didn't answer his sister's greeting.

"What's wrong?" Lali asked. She knew her brother well.

"What? Wrong? Nothing's wrong," Yoni snapped nervously. He distractedly stroked Amalia, and got a nip on his finger. "Ouch." He shook his hand. "Why are you doing that to me?"

"What am I doing?"

"Not you. Amalia. She bit me."

"She wants you to treat her nicely," Lali defended her brother's bird. "And I can tell that something happened to you in cheder today."

"Something," Yoni said. He did not look very interested in sharing with his little sister. Lali, who remembered that she wanted to help her brothers fulfill their dreams, made a mental note of the fact that Yoni was angry. Maybe, by making his dream come true, she could make him happy?

"Fine, so if you want to really know," Yoni told her harshly. He was acting as if he was angry about Lali prying, but deep down he was actually happy that someone was taking an interest in him, "I fought with Dovi."

Lali was quiet. Actually, she was stunned. Her jaw dropped. Yoni? Fought? With Dovi?

"Close your mouth," Yoni snapped. "Otherwise flies might get in."

"Why did you fight with him?"

"Because," Yoni answered. "And that's it. You wanted to know, now you know. So just be busy with your lamb and be quiet."

Lali didn't think she deserved this reaction, but she couldn't blame a little kid who had fought with his best and only friend. She took the lamb back to its pen and slipped quietly away.

"Ah...." Lali said as everything became crystal clear, "Yoni's dream is to make up with Dovi."

Again, Lali called her sisters for a meeting. They were very happy with the outcome of the operation for Ayala, and were willing to come again — mostly because they were also very curious.

"I'm not sure," Miri said slowly. "First we need to find out what they fought about."

"Doesn't he want to make up?" Etty asked. "What difference does it make what they fought about?"

"It's possible that Yoni is angry, or offended, and he doesn't yet want to make up with his friend who hurt him or got him angry," Chani explained.

"We need to find out, that's the first thing," Miri wrote in her notebook. She raised her eyes. "Who is volunteering to do that?"

## Chapter 28

# The Reason for the Fight

The girls were quiet. None of them were very excited about the idea of going to speak with Yoni about what caused the fight with his friend. They were all sure that Yoni would become as prickly as an angry porcupine, and wouldn't want to answer any questions. Who would muster up the courage to talk to him?

"You, Lali," said Etty. "You're the best for the job."

"Not fair!" Lali grumbled. "I told you everything, and I arranged everything, why should I be the one to ask him?"

"Because you organized it and told us," Etty argued.

"Not true! I also asked him that question already, and he already got annoyed at me, so now it's someone else's turn!" Lali argued heatedly.

"You're right about that," Etty admitted. After a minute of thinking, she said bravely, "Fine, I'll ask him."

"Yes? Okay, great." Miri marked down in her book:

*Done by: Etty*

"The second job is to see what will lower the flames between the two," Chani said in her flowery language.

"Flames?" Lali was puzzled. "Which flames?" She'd had enough with the two fires she had witnessed — at her aunt's house in Be'er Sheva, and the fire in their house caused by the mirrors Yoni had put up.

"It's an expression," Chani explained. "We have to check how we can strike a compromise between them. And we can only do that after we hear what the fight is all about."

Miri closed her notebook with a snap. "This meeting is adjourned," she said officially, "until the results of the investigation by Esther Schneider."

Everyone looked at Etty with admiration, and she felt very important indeed. She set out for her secret mission, and as she went, wondered how she would take care of the important task her sisters had entrusted her with.

She couldn't ask Yoni directly. He wouldn't give her a normal answer. She needed to go ask…wait! Shoshi, her classmate! She was Dovi's sister! Maybe Dovi wasn't as secretive as Yoni, and had told his sister that he had a fight with Yoni, and maybe he had also told her what the fight was about?!

She hurried to call, without planning properly by preparing what to ask. "Hello, Shoshi?"

"Yes?" Shoshi was a bit surprised, because Etty was not one of her good friends.

"What—" Etty began to understand that her question would sound a bit strange. So she decided to bypass the subject. "What…what's doing?"

"Fine, *baruch Hashem*." Shoshi waited to hear what this was about.

"How are you doing?"

"*Baruch Hashem*." Shoshi was taken aback, but didn't say anything of course.

"And…what's going on?"

"Nothing." Shoshi thought that Etty sounded a bit strange.

"What's new?"

"Nothing new." Shoshi was too polite to ask Etty direct-ly, "What do you want?"

"How...is the whole family?" Etty was very annoyed at herself now. Why hadn't she just asked Yoni and finished? Was she afraid of him? What was Shoshi thinking of her by now?

"Everyone is fine," Shoshi said, and wondered if Etty herself was feeling okay. Maybe she needed help? "Are you okay?" she finally asked.

"Yes, I'm fine," Etty said, a bit too firmly, because Shoshi retreated.

"Sorry. If you don't feel well, I can hang up."

"No, I'm fine. Tell me, everyone in your house is feeling okay? All your brothers?"

"I only have one brother."

"And he's alright?" Etty grasped the opportunity.

"Why not?"

Etty didn't know where to go from there, so she coughed for a long moment. Shoshi was now convinced that Etty didn't feel well. "Are you sure you're feeling alright?" she asked.

"Yes, I'm fine," Etty stopped coughing. Uch! Where would this stupid conversation go now? How had she gotten into this? "I'll tell you." She finally chose to go with the truth. "My brother is friends with your brother."

"Oh!" Shoshi realized right away. "You mean the story with the pit?"

"What?"

"You know, with the pit, that Dovi fell into...."

Etty listened to the story. Apparently, Dovi was not as secretive as Yoni, and he had told his sister exactly what had caused the fight.

This is what seems to have happened:

Dovi and Yoni made up to play in the cheder yard. Yoni was the one who suggested an interesting ball game that his sisters had taught him. The advantage of the game was that they didn't need lots of boys. That was great for Yoni, because he didn't like lots of ruckus and noise. And also, it didn't take a lot of skill.

Dovi agreed and they went down to the yard. Yoni chose a quiet corner, near the gate. Dovi stood a few feet away and Yoni held the ball.

"Now we need to run," Yoni instructed his friend. "I throw it, and you catch it, and then I run to the place where you were. After that, you stand with the ball and wait for me to come. Got it?"

Dovi got it and began to run quickly. But almost as soon as he took off, he suddenly slipped and disappeared from Yoni's view. Poof! He was gone!

Yoni gaped in shock. A minute ago, there had been a boy there, and now he wasn't there anymore! Where had he gone?! Had he risen On High like Eliyahu Hanavi, l'havdil? Had the ground opened up beneath him, like Korach? He almost began to scream in fear, but first he decided to check it out. With trembling knees, he came closer to the place where Dovi had disappeared. And what did he see? Dovi's head peeking out from…nowhere; Dovi came up from the dirt, like a carrot growing in the ground, like a mole coming out of its den. But as opposed to the carrot and the mole, which come out of the ground quietly, Dovi emerged with thunder and lightning….

## Chapter 29

# The Pit of Dispute

"Tell me, are you normal?!" Dovi shrieked, his face covered with sand, his teeth, *peyos*, lips, yarmulke — all a mess of sand and dust. "How could you do such a thing to me?!"

"Me?" Yoni bristled. "What did I do?"

"Don't ask me, what did I do?! You brought me here on purpose to make me fall into this pit!!!"

"Me??" Now Yoni was not only offended, but he also recoiled in shock. "What are you talking about?! How could you think such a thing about me?!"

"Of course I think!" Dovi fumed. "You never want to go out to the yard, and all of a sudden today you wanted to. You chose this place on purpose, and then told me to run right on this path! Is this some kind of a bad joke?! Well, lemme tell you. It's not a joke! It's…it's…it's…." He couldn't find the right words so he ended off with, "It's the opposite of a joke!"

"But I didn't do it!" Yoni defended himself. "Really, I didn't!"

"Tell it to the judge!" Dovi shouted angrily as he tried (and failed) to get himself out of the pit. Every time he tried to clamber up, he just set loose more dirt and fell in deeper. "Maybe you can help me out of here?!"

Yoni hesitated for a minute. Dovi had insulted him deeply, and now he was asking for help?

"I don't want to," he refused, shrugging. "You're accusing me and I didn't do anything! You're suspecting an innocent person. That's called *choshed b'kesheirim.* And now you're asking for help?"

"I am not being *choshed b'kesheirim*! I'm suspecting—" Again he spluttered, looking for the right word, and said, "Not *kesheirim*, that's for sure!"

"I *am* honest and I *am* innocent," Yoni said indignantly. "I had no idea this pit was here, I promise! And you're just accusing me without finding out!"

"I don't believe you," Dovi said bluntly. "After your joke failed, you say that it's not you. You planned it!" He slipped a little further inside, and set off another shower of stones and dirt.

"I did not plan it," Yoni felt the weight of the accusation that he was not guilty of. Dovi did look quite funny: he was immersed in sand, his eyes were sparking with fury, and his *peyos* were all mussed. But Yoni was not thinking about the humorous side of things.

"It's not the truth. It's...it's...." Dovi searched for a word. "Not the truth!" he concluded.

"It is absolutely the truth," Yoni declared. "And I'll help you get out of there even though you are accusing me. But only because I feel bad for you."

"You feel bad for me?" Dovi sneered. "That's not—"But he didn't add a word because just then, a few small pebbles tumbled into the pit and landed in his mouth. "Phew... ich...argg..." he groaned, spitting out the pebbles.

"So you don't want me to help you?" Yoni needled.

"No need. I'll manage on my own." Dovi attempted to heave himself out of the pit, his hands scrabbling for something to grab on to. He didn't find anything but

a few small stones, and as he grabbed at them, they slipped away from him. He found himself falling into the sand over and over, climbing an inch and then slipping back. His heart was bursting with anger over what his friend had done.

Yoni moved away from the whole scene. Every so often, he stole a glance behind him, because his kind heart did not allow him to stare at Dovi struggling.

After efforts, grunts, failed attempts, and lots of slipping and sliding, Dovi was finally out of the pit. He was in a sour mood, and covered with dirt and sand from the top of his head to his shoes, and everywhere in between. He staggered toward the principal's office, leaving a trail of sand behind him. He had to speak to the principal to make sure it was filled. More children could fall in, and it was literally a pit in a public area, a *bor birshus harabbim*, in the simplest sense. Children could be hurt, or could even break something; even if that didn't happen, they could be frightened. If a first-grade boy, or even worse, a boy from the preschool, would fall in there, he could become terribly frightened! He might even disappear and wouldn't be able to get out! Oh, the trouble that Yoni had caused when he dug that pit....

Dovi walked into the principal's office. Of course, the principal was stunned to see a huge chunk of dirt standing in front of him; Dovi was so covered that the principal could not even figure out who it was.

"Who are you?"

"Dovi," the brown thing answered. He looked like he had just emerged from the desert. "I want to tell the *menahel* that there is a pit in the yard, and someone could fall in." He generously decided to leave out Yoni's part in this incident, so that he shouldn't get punished.

"Yes, yes, I know. It's from the electric company. They didn't fill it? They promised that they would! I told them it's dangerous and I see that I was right, and you fell in," the principal said to the brown chunk in front of him.

The room spun around Dovi. "Electric company?!" He had blamed Yoni for no reason.

"Yes. Go home and get washed up and changed," the principal suggested. "Thank you for being responsible and coming to tell me about it."

"Okay," Dovi said dejectedly. "Thank you."

With a heavy heart, he left the room. What would Yoni say to all those accusations he'd hurled at him?

Yoni didn't say anything. Dovi didn't have the courage to apologize, or explain that he had found out that Yoni was not to blame. Why hadn't he done some investigating before accusing Yoni? He knew that this wasn't the kind of thing that Yoni would do. And yet Dovi had been so sure...and so angry....

So Yoni didn't say anything and Dovi didn't explain, and since then, the two good friends hadn't spoken with each other at all.

## Chapter 30

### Dove of Peace

"Is that it?" Etty asked. "I can take care of this in one minute." She fought and made up with her friends so often that she didn't understand how Yoni could fight without making up right away.

"Really?" Shoshi asked hopefully. "How?" Dovi was sad and dejected, and he seemed to feel guilty. Shoshi felt bad for him and wanted to bring an end to this fight as soon as possible.

Etty thought about it. How could she mediate between the two? "Let me talk to my sisters," she told Shoshi. "I'm sure they'll have a good idea. I'll let you know later."

By then Etty felt that she'd completed her serious detective work, and she'd leave the rest of the job to her smarter sisters. Again, the Schneider girls' committee was called to the peace council.

"What's the deal?" Riki asked curiously. "Why were the boys fighting?"

Etty briefly told them the story of the pit, and finished with Shoshi's hope that it would soon be resolved.

The girls sat and thought.

"Dovi needs to apologize," Riki decided. "That much is clear. He blamed Yoni for something he didn't do! One who is *choshed beksheirim* gets a blow to his body!"

"And that's what happened to him," Chani snickered. "He fell into a pit!"

"That happened afterwards. First he got the blow and then he suspected an innocent person," Miri pointed out.

"And don't forget that he had lots of reasons to suspect Yoni. He never wants to go out to play, and then he led him straight to the pit," Etty explained.

"Without meaning to!" Miri exclaimed.

"Yes, but he didn't know that. It looked too planned," Etty defended her brother's friend.

"Fine, but he should have found out the details before attacking like that," Miri defended her brother.

"*Nu*, we know that. That's the whole point. But Dovi is embarrassed to apologize. It's hard to ask for forgiveness, after you screamed and accused someone." Etty also understood Dovi.

"He could write a letter," Chani said. She loved to write, as we know. "It's easier to write a letter than apologize face to face."

"Who should write? Yoni?" Shevi asked. "He has nothing to write about!"

"Not Yoni, Dovi!"

"Dovi should write? What will he write?"

"He'll apologize, and explain why he thought it was Yoni, and he'll explain that the principal told him that it was really the electric company."

"I don't think Dovi needs that idea. He probably already thought of writing a letter, but he just doesn't have the courage to do it," Shevi mused aloud.

"Well, he has to do something."

"Someone needs to help him take the first step."

"Who, us?"

"Yes," Etty said with confidence. "Shoshi and I. We need to mediate between them. Yes, yes, to mediate." She enjoyed the word.

"Do you have an idea of how to mediate?"

"It's hard work," Etty sighed. "Does anyone have an idea how we can mediate between Yoni and Dovi?"

"I have one," Lali said slowly. "An amazing idea."

"What?" Miri, Chani, and Riki asked in unison.

"Simple. We'll send him a carrier pigeon."

"To Dovi????"

"No. To Yoni."

"How to Yoni? He has the birds!" Miri was surprised.

"We'll give Dovi one bird," Lali explained her idea. "And we'll tell him to attach a letter to it. Yoni can't ignore a letter sent to him through one of his own carrier pigeons!"

The idea was brilliant from all angles. Indeed, it was flawless. Dovi wouldn't refuse to participate in such an adventure, especially if it would get him his friend back!

"Who will bring him the pigeon?" Etty asked carefully. "We need to take it in the afternoon, after Yoni feeds it, so that he won't notice that it's gone. Then, in the evening when he comes back, it needs to arrive."

"I'll take it," Lali volunteered. "After all, I'm taking care of my lammy at that time. Yoni won't suspect anything if I stay after he feeds the pigeons."

"I'll talk to Shoshi," Etty concluded, "and we'll get Dovi to agree. Dovi will write a letter, and he'll give it to his sister Shoshi. At about four or five, Lali will bring the pigeon to Dovi's house, and will attach the letter Shoshi gives her to the bird. Then she'll send it from Dovi's house to ours!"

"Lali! Look!" Yoni could not believe his eyes when he saw his Amalia returning one evening, and in her beak was...a letter!"

Lali suppressed a knowing smile. "Really?!" asked innocently. "A pigeon? Yours?"

"Yes, it's Amalia, look at the mark!"

Lali hid her smile in Buma's wool. "Yes, yes, I see! When did she disappear?"

"I didn't notice," Yoni admitted. "But now she's back.... So when did she go?"

"That is strange," agreed Lali. "Maybe open the letter and you'll see?"

Yoni opened the letter with sparkling eyes and trembling fingers. His eyes scanned the lines.

To my dear friend, Yoni.

I'm very sorry for insulting you.

I later found out from the menahel that you were not to blame. It was the electric company's fault. I just felt like a fox who had slipped into a snake hole, like a fish that fell into a net, like a radish that fell into a salad

So I hope you'll understand me and forgive me.

Your good friend, Dovi.

PS The principal said that the electric company closed up the pit that same day because it was very dangerous.

Yoni held the letter in his hand, and his face turned red. Lali stole a peek, and only when she saw the big grin crossing his face did she relax a bit. Yoni put Amalia in the coop and hurried back into the house. She strained her ears and managed to hear him call out, "Ima, I'm going to Dovi, okay?"

And that's how she knew that their mission had been accomplished.

## Chapter 31

### *The Performance*

"A performance!" Riki burst into the house with a triumphant shout. "A performance!"

"What? When?" Ima, who was serving lunch to the twins, turned her head to her daughter. Tammy used that moment to turn the bowl with her soup over her head.

"*Oy vey!*" Riki exclaimed. "Look what she did, mischief maker!"

Tammy wore the soup bowl like a hat, and looked very pleased with herself. Orange liquid had splattered on the kitchen walls, on her high chair, and on Eli's high chair. Rivers of orange flowed down her forehead. She looked like a little, chubby, laughing sweet potato.

"*Oy vey* is right," Ima agreed. "I'll go bathe her. Do you want to clean up the kitchen a bit or feed Eli?"

"I'll feed Eli," Riki volunteered.

"And I'll clean up the kitchen," Shevi volunteered. She'd wandered into the kitchen after her sister. "Did you hear about the performance, Ima?"

"I'm hearing about it now," Ima said as she held Tammy, who continued waving her soupy spoon around, now spraying orange drops on Riki's and Shevi's faces.

"It's a performance! With the whole school!" Riki exclaimed excitedly to Eli as she kept spooning him the soup. Eli leaned forward and grabbed Riki's glasses with both hands.

"'Lasses," he said proudly when he saw his sister's shocked face. Shevi burst out laughing, pried the glasses out of his hands, and put them back on her sister's nose.

"What happened to you?" Miri walked into the kitchen and saw her sisters speckled with orange drops. "Did you drop into a room that was being painted orange?"

"No, Tammy sprayed us with soup," the two explained. "Did you hear about the performance?" Riki added.

"Sure." Miri's face lit up. She, like Riki, also hoped to get a big part. This was no little skit for their class. This was the real thing, with costumes, scenery, and a big screen on the stage!

When Tammy came back, all washed up, Miri and Riki took turns telling their mother about the upcoming performance.

"There will be real costumes, and a director!" Riki cried.

"And all the mothers are going to be invited," Miri explained.

"Some girls will be in the choir or dance, but there will also be girls putting on the play," Etty added as she entered the kitchen.

"And I want so much to be in the play!" Riki was dramatic, as usual.

"And I don't," Chani and Shevi said together.

"Whatever you choose is fine with me," Ima said with a smile, studying her daughters.

"It's all in honor of the school's twenty-fifth anniversary," Riki explained. She rinsed her face with water, and cleaned her glasses. "That's why they are doing it."

"I want to write the newspaper that's going to come out for the occasion," Chani said hopefully.

"And I want to be in dance," Etty said.

"And I want the play," Miri and Riki said in unison.

"What about you, Shevi?"

"I haven't decided yet. I might want to be in the choir."

"The main thing is that the whole school is part of it," Ima said with satisfaction. "I'm happy that everyone is happy."

"But I'm not happy yet, Ima," Riki warned her mother. "Because they only choose one girl in each class for the play. I'm not sure that I'll be chosen."

"Well, I hope that I *will* be chosen."

"So now we have to wait, count the days, and pray," Chani said using her usual flowery language.

"And do homework," Ima announced. "Let's go, girls!"

The girls headed to do homework. Only Lali was missing, but that was no wonder. From the minute she returned home until supper, she was busy with her lamb.

"I was chosen!!!" Riki shrieked as she stormed into the house the next day. "Ima!!!"

"Really?! That's wonderful!" Ima was thrilled for her daughter. "I davened for you this morning. Was Miri chosen?"

"Yes! That was going to happen anyway, because her friends said she's perfect for it. But I wasn't sure about me."

"You can never be sure." Ima smiled at her delighted daughter, who was ready to hug the whole world. Lali slipped away with a mysterious smile. She had given five shekels to tzedakah and said the whole *Yom Shlishi* in *Tehillim* for her sister. After all, she'd promised that she would help her family realize their dreams, right? Ayala's and Yoni's dreams had come true; it was Riki's turn. And how could she have helped her if not by *davening* and giving tzedakah?

Chani was chosen to write the newspaper, of course, because who in her class was better for the job? And Etty was chosen for the dance, as she'd wanted. Shevi was in choir. Only Lali's attitude toward the whole thing was very casual. She hadn't been picked for any special role but hadn't wanted one in the first place. She didn't think that a play could compare to an important real, live lamb.

Chani, Etty, and Shevi were happy with their parts, but you couldn't compare their happiness and excitement to that of Miri and Riki. At first, there had been elections for each job, and then there was the tense waiting and the excitement. There were a few big roles, and many girls really wanted them. On the first day, Miri was chosen for a pretty big part. She was in three scenes, and was very happy.

Only on the second day were the younger girls called to get their parts. Until then, Riki could hardly breathe. She was too excited. Her whole family was waiting to hear the decision.

Riki came home shining like the midday sun.

She had been chosen for one of the four main parts!

From that day on, the only thing anyone talked about in the Schneider house was the performance.

## Chapter 32

### *Practice*

"I'll practice and you'll listen," Riki told her twin. "It has to be very convincing. I'm a little Jewish girl trying to escape from the convent after she finds out that her aunt is looking for her. The nun tries to stop her and bring her back to the convent."

"But isn't the play a secret?" Shevi asked. "My teacher said to keep it a surprise."

"Yes, but you have to help me practice," Riki explained. "How will I know it by heart if you don't?"

"And the director lets?" Shevi asked, in her very honest way. Her inner conscience guided her through everything she did.

"Yes. I even asked her. She said it's fine if each girl finds someone to help her practice. But only one! She doesn't want every girl in the school to know the whole play — because every time the girl practiced she did it with someone else."

"Okay," Shevi agreed. She listened curiously to the lines of little Clara, who was in the convent, and whose heart yearned to rejoin her brethren outside the convent walls. Then Clara met with her aunt, Rivka, her mother's sister, who told her about her life before the war and revealed that she was Jewish. It was all so emotional!

"Okay, turn to page two," Riki instructed her sister.

Shevi turned the pages that were marked. "Here it is. It starts with the words, 'I don't remember'?"

"Yes, that's it. Now, let's start. I don't remember my mother so well," Riki began in a sweet, sad voice. "Or my father. But if you remind me, I'll remember. I do remember how Tatte used to sing 'Shalom Aleichem.' Do you know the tune?"

Shevi, standing in for the aunt, answered by reading from the pages. "Yes, I do know it. It was a special tune that Zeide composed. Do you want to hear? Like this…." Shevi paused. "The aunt is supposed to sing now?"

"Yes. Don't keep stopping every minute. Sing Shalom Aleichem."

"But I don't know the Zeide's tune!" Shevi was at a loss.

"It doesn't matter. Sing what Abba sings."

"Fine." Shevi hummed the tune that most people used. "*Shalom aleichem malachei hashares, malachi elyon….*"

"Yes, yes, that's the tune! How do you know it?"

"Because he was also my Zeide, Clara, my dear. I remember how my sister, your mother, held you in her arms when you were little, and sang to you."

"I want to go to Mamme! To Tatte! Take me with you!"

"We can't go to Mamme," Shevi said, and her eyes filled with tears. "Tatte and Mamme are in Shamayim, looking down at you. Do you want to come with me to a place where there are only Jews?"

"Yes, but Sister Marie doesn't let—"

"You'll need to tell her that you want to. Even if she shouts at you, and even if she punishes you, it will be worth it, right, my dear *neshamah*?"

"Yes, Aunt Rivka, yes."

"That's it," Shevi said. "Then it's the next scene."

"Fine," Riki said. "Skip to the part with the nun. Can you

see it? Page twelve."

Shevi turned the pages. "Got it."

"Good, start."

"How dare you?? How do you dare say such a thing?"

"Because…Aunt Rivka."

"I will not let you go to the Jews there under any circumstances. We saved your body, and we're going to save your soul as well! And don't be tempted by all of her promises and sweet-sounding words!" Shevi didn't even realize she was talking in the tone of an angry nun.

"I want to go to my people—"

"You don't belong there anymore! And if you try to run away, you'll be severely punished!"

"Did you hear that?" Bentzy, sitting and listening to the sisters, heard Riki pleading and weeping, and he got very angry.

"What?" Shuey, who was counting his *rabbanim* pictures, hadn't heard a thing.

"In a few days, a scary nun is going to come and scream

at our Riki that she won't let her belong to the Jewish nation! Did you ever hear of such a thing?"

"Who told you? And how do you even know what a nun is?"

"What do you mean, who told me? Don't you hear what is happening around you? For two weeks, Riki has been crying about it every day! She sits with Shevi and cries that the scary nun is going to come and take her!"

"To the convent?" Shuey's eyes widened in fear and horror.

"Yes! And you're sitting here quietly?!"

"I didn't know," Shuey tried to ward off his brother's anger. "I didn't know anything! How did such a thing happen? And Abba and Ima don't know about it?"

"I guess not," replied Bentzy.

"Then shouldn't we tell them about it?" Shuey asked. In his eyes, this was the best solution. After all, is there any problem an Ima or Abba can't solve?

"But if Riki didn't tell them, then she for sure has a reason," Bentzy reasoned aloud. "Maybe the nun is threatening her that if she tells her parents, she'll catch them, too? I'm sure that if Riki could have told Ima about this already, she would have."

Bentzy's words made sense. It was clear to both boys that as soon as Riki could, she would tell her parents right away about the very difficult situation she was in.

"So what are we going to do?" Shuey fretted. He pushed his pictures aside. He was too worried to deal with them. "We have to do something to save her!"

"I have an idea!" Bentzy exclaimed. "We'll go there with a false identity, and when she has to go meet the scary nun, we'll just take her and run away!"

## Chapter 33

### *The Costume*

"What are you thinking about so much?" Sruly asked his younger brother when he found him once again standing on with one foot on the floor, his eyes gazing into space. This was the fourth time he'd found him in this strange position, and he wanted to know what it was about.

Shuey put his other foot down with a sigh. "About our false identities that didn't work out," he said honestly. "Did you hear about that story?"

Ayala had decided not to share that story with anyone in order to preserve her brothers' dignity. So Sruly shook his head. "Nope. I don't know anything."

"So listen." Shuey's eyes lit up when he began to tell the story. He skipped the unpleasant parts, like flying shoes.

"Ayala told us what a false identity is. When you make up that you're fake, not really you. We were very excited, so Tully and I traded identities."

"We did that once, when each one went to his brother's class to solve his problems." Sruly waved it off.

"No, no," Shuey protested. "That's something else. Completely different. I want to dress up!" He didn't say for what. Bentzy said it was a surprise and supposed to be a secret. If Riki hadn't shared her problem with anyone, then she certainly had a good reason.

"Me, too," Sruly agreed. "I already told Ima that this year I'm getting dressed up as a gorilla! She doesn't like gorillas much, but maybe she'll agree, because Shimmy and—"

"Who's talking about Purim?!" Shuey grumbled. "I am not talking about a Purim costume! I want a real costume!"

"What is a real costume?" Sruly was taken aback. "If it's real, it's not a costume!"

"You don't understand," Shuey said with patience that he did not usually show. "The costume of a real person!"

"Ah. Like, Mordechai HaYehudi, who was real? Or like Rav Ovadia Yosef?"

"No!" Shuey was fuming. "In a costume so they won't know who I am. More like if I get dressed up like a *bochur*, or a *melamed* in cheder, or the man from the grocery."

"You can't be any of those," Sruly declared. "Because with your height, you're still going to look like a boy. No matter what you wear everyone will still know that you are a boy."

Shuey was offended, and annoyed. "Who says?" he snapped. "If I get dressed up, everyone might think I'm an old man who shrank!"

"An old man shrinks?" Sruly wrinkled his forehead, puzzled.

"Yes, if there's someone tall, when he gets old, slowly he gets shorter."

"Maybe a bit," Sruly said, minimizing the whole issue. "But no old man is the size of a boy. It makes no sense."

"It has to make sense," Shuey insisted. "I need people to think that I'm an adult."

"Maybe you should walk on cans?" Sruly laughed. "Or on broomsticks."

"That's a good idea," Shuey exclaimed. Sruly was joking

but Shuey took him seriously. "I just need to see how I manage with the shoes and the pants so it doesn't look weird."

"Just forget it," Sruly hurried to talk Shuey out of the idea. "It won't work. You can't lift up cans of pickles with every step you take. They're very heavy. And besides, your face is very boyish."

"My face won't look like a boy's face," Shuey said mysteriously. "Wait and see."

The whole next day, Shuey and Bentzy worked on Shuey's costume. They had decided that they would put all their efforts into one costume, because time was very short. They needed to save Riki quickly! Riki had said it was all happening the day after tomorrow! Soon their sister whom they loved would stand in front of the threatening nun, and her life would be on the line. That's what they heard her saying. So Shuey, wearing Abba's clothes, would be the one to save her.

Bentzy and Shuey worked to glue two cans to one another. Why two? Because when Shuey stood on one can of pickles, they saw that he was not tall enough. The two cans together gave him the right height.

"It's ready," Bentzy said. He had carefully glued the empty can of pickles that he'd found in the garbage to a full can of olives. "Do you see what a miracle it is that I found the empty can? This way it won't be too heavy for you — schlepping two full cans with every step."

"Glue them very tight," Shuey said a bit worriedly. The whole thing didn't look stable enough to him.

"How are you going to put shoes on this?"

"I'll use Abba's old shoes," Shuey explained. "We'll stick the can into the shoe. No one will know that the other half of the shoe is empty."

"Great idea," Bentzy complimented. "Come, get on the can and we'll see if it's okay."

"The cans, not one can," Shuey corrected. He stepped onto the tower, supported by Bentzy and…fell onto the floor, together with both cans.

"Ouch!! Owwww!" poor Shuey shrieked as the cans separated, rolled around, and smashed his hand, after he fell onto the floor. "What did you glue them with?"

"Regular white glue," Bentzy said apologetically. "I

thought it would be strong enough."

"No! It's not strong enough! It's not strong at all!" He stopped himself from showering his brother with all sorts of choice names. "Take clear tape and finish a whole roll on these cans! That's the only way to connect them!"

"Too bad you didn't say that in the first place," Bentzy murmured. He was sad about his tower of cans that had crashed.

"It is too bad." Shuey rubbed his fingers. "My fingers wouldn't have gotten hurt."

## Chapter 34

# The Children Dress Up

Bentzy did as he was told, and used an entire roll of tape to connect the two cans — the full one and the empty one. Now Shuey could be sure that his little tower would hold his weight. At least he hoped it would.

Shuey leaned on Bentzy and climbed onto the tower. Now he was the right height, and his eyes sparkled. "All I need are shoes like Abba's, and a beard with a mustache," he said. "No one will realize that I'm a boy."

Bentzy was a bit doubtful. "Your face is small."

"You're just like Sruly." Shuey was offended. "Everything is fine with my face."

"Of course your face is fine, if it is the face of a boy your age," Bentzy agreed. "But as Abba's face...I don't know if it's enough."

"I'm a short, skinny Abba," Shuey said firmly. "And don't go and ruin anything."

"I'm going to get Abba's shoes," Bentzy said. "Will you figure out the suit and the beard and mustache?"

"Yes." Shuey held the glue tightly. "Just hurry." His fingers still ached, and they had to finish getting the costume ready. Now they were going to try it on to see if it was all right.

*Everything seems to be okay*, Shuey thought to himself as he put a bit of the glue on his socks. He was going to stand on the cans in only his socks. Because if he tried to put on his shoes the pants could not hide them. They would stick out like a pair of electric poles on a flat road. Or like two kneidlach in clear chicken soup.

"I can bend my feet like this," Shuey showed Bentzy. "But not the shoes. They're too stubborn."

The socks were glued to the cans, and Shuey clomped around proudly on his cans. No one would believe that he wasn't someone! Or rather, that he was someone! He was the right height! Now he'd paste on the beard and mustache that Ima had bought them for Purim, when they'd dressed up as a baker and a shoemaker from the shtetl, and the costume would be perfect. Even then, Savta had said that he looked so much like Abba. If he would be Abba's height, no one would realize that he was a boy.

He carefully smeared glue on the beard, and waited a few minutes, like the instructions told him to. Then he pressed it to his face. Uch…it did *not* feel comfortable. The glue stung his skin, but he tried to ignore it and focus on his important goal. By the time he glued the mustache on he was less enthusiastic, because his skin was still burning a bit.

Bentzy entered the room, and was quite impressed. "You look great!" he gushed. "No one would believe that you are Shuey! You look like a real *abba*!"

Shuey sat down heavily on the chair. Bentzy tried to put Abba's old shoes on the cans. When he stood up, everything looked very good: the long suit covered Shuey's feet that were jutting out of the pants. He was the right height.

"Give me a hand," Shuey said. "It's a bit hard to walk with all this."

"Tomorrow you'll have to go yourself."

"That's why I'm practicing today."

Slowly, like an old man with a white beard, and not like a young man with a black beard — like the one Shuey had glued on — Shuey walked toward the stairs. He put out one foot, while his other foot got caught on the long suit he was wearing.

Shuey lost his balance and missed one step. He went tumbling down the stairs.

"Ohohohoh!! Ahhhhh! Help! Help! Help!" poor Shuey hollered. Bentzy, who was supporting him, also tripped, but he managed to stick his hand out and grab the banister, so he didn't fall all the way down.

Tangled in the long suit, his feet pasted to the cans, and his hands waving in the air, Shuey couldn't stop his tumble down the stairs. He landed at Ima's feet, still screaming.

"Wh...wh...what?" Even Ima, who was used to unbelievable scenes, was gaping at this strange creature. "Wh..what happened?"

"Owww!!! I fell!!" Shuey cried loudly, ignoring the fact that he was suddenly "a father."

"Falling is just the end of the story," Ima said with a

sympathetic but stern look on her face. She reached out and helped Shuey get up. "What is this beard? And the mustache? Is it Purim today?" She tried to remove the mustache from Shuey's face, but he shrieked: "Owww! You can't take it off!"

"Why?" Ima was surprised. "Is it your mustache?"

"Yes, it's mine!"

"I mean, did it grow on your face, so I can't take it off?"

"No, I grew it with glue!"

"Come quickly, let's try to take it off," Ima said, in alarm. "It will hurt if we wait too much longer."

Ima helped Shuey to his feet, or rather helped him to his cans. When she did she was shocked to see that he was almost her height. "What happened to you?!" Had her dear son grown up overnight?

"I tried," Shuey — mustache, beard and all — sobbed, "to save Riki—"

"To save me?" Riki had come running when she heard her name. "What do you mean?"

"What don't you understand?" Shuey snapped. "Yes, yes, to save you!"

"To save me? From who?"

"From the scary nun!"

It took Riki a long moment to understand. And then she burst into a shriek of laughter that shook the whole house. It even scared Yoni's pigeons and Lali's lamb. "Ha-ha-ha," she laughed, wiping tears from her eyes. "You thought it was real?"

"It's not real?" Shuey began to realize that something wasn't as he had understood it to be.

"No! It's a play!"

"A play?"

"Yes, a play!"

"Fine," Shuey said, disappointed. He was still wearing the suit, the beard, and the mustache. "But always remember that we wanted to save you. And if you ever need us, we'll come!"

## Chapter 35

# *The Understudy*

Riki got up the next morning super excited. "Today is the final rehearsal!" she exclaimed. "With mothers and friends in the audience! And tomorrow — is the real thing! Can you believe it?" She washed her hands, still dizzy with excitement.

"No, I can't," Shevi admitted as she stretched. "All these weeks of practice…. Are you happy it's going to be over?"

"A bit yes and a lot no," Riki said. Her voice was still hoarse from sleep.

"What's in the bit of yes and what's in the lot of no?" asked Shevi.

"In the bit of yes is the pressure that I feel from the play, that everything should go perfectly. That I shouldn't mess up my lines or fall or stammer. And the lots of no is that I'll be sorry that the rehearsals are over and all the good fun things that had to do with the rehearsals will also finish."

"Well," Shevi declared, "all of life is actually like that. Good things finish, just like bad things do. Just cough a bit, because you are hoarse."

Riki coughed and tried to talk. "Is it better now?"

"No, it's worse," Shevi said worriedly. "Go eat a raw egg."

"Oy!" Riki gasped. "Why would I do something like that?"

"Because raw eggs help you get your voice back! Go drink something."

Riki disappeared. Shevi waited for her to come back, fretting the whole time as she slowly got dressed. Was everything okay with her twin?

"*Nu?*" she asked when Riki came back. "Is everything okay with your voice?"

"No," Riki shook her head, tears in her eyes. "It's only getting worse." Her voice was getting hoarser with each word she spoke.

"It's probably because you're so excited," Shevi said. "Relax. You know that you know your part perfectly and everything is fine. And you'll see that all of it — including your voice — will be good."

"I don't know," Riki whispered. Her face looked very worried. "I can't talk at all." Her voice was barely a whisper.

Shevi looked at her sister in horror. "What's going to be?"

Riki shrugged, and her eyes, which were filled with tears, began to drip.

Shevi reached out, took her sister's hand, and squeezed it tightly, without words. Ima entered the room with a worried look. "What's doing, Riki?"

Riki pointed to her throat and whispered, "I can't talk."

"But today," Ima sounded very concerned, "is the dress rehearsal for the mothers, on stage! You—" She stopped herself. What could she say. 'You can't not come?' If Hashem had decided that Riki would be hoarse, then she wouldn't be able to go!

"And tomorrow," Shevi said even more worriedly, "is the real show! What's going to be?"

Abba also came into the twins' room, and in his soothing voice he said, "Riki, I think you need to rest today and not go to the dress rehearsal."

"It's not a dress rehearsal," Shevi explained agitatedly. "It's also a real performance! All the girls' mothers are coming! And the whole school! It's almost the real thing!"

Abba's forehead creased and he exchanged a glance with Ima. "We'll see what can be done. Meanwhile, girls, get dressed and ready."

And they left the room.

"If you don't come today, what are they going to do?" Shevi sounded aghast.

Riki whispered. "Every actress has an understudy. Someone who learned the lines like her. And if she can't come, then the understudy performs instead of her."

"Great!" Shevi exclaimed. "So today, the understudy will come in your place, and tomorrow, you'll be there!"

"No, no," Riki whispered miserably. "If the understudy performs today, then she's going to perform tomorrow, too! Because the director wants to see exactly how it's going to be tomorrow."

Shevi bit her bottom lip. "So what are you going to do?"

"I can't *not* go today," Riki said, and wept quietly. Shevi's heart was breaking with pity for her twin. What would be? What could she do? She had an idea, but it was so… so…not like her, that she could barely say it. She was the total opposite of this idea, but for her sister…maybe… maybe….

"I have an idea," she said slowly.

Riki raised her wet eyes. "What?"

"I'll go instead of you today."

Riki gaped at her sister, as if she'd told her she was planning to join a hunting trip for polar bears to the North Pole. "What???" she croaked.

"I know the part, I learned it. I just need…to…overcome my embarrassment. If I perform today, then you can perform tomorrow."

Riki could not believe what a good heart Shevi had. Shevi was an amazing actress; they had both seen that. Would she really get on stage and act in front of hundreds of women and girls?

"You…you…would?"

"It will be hard for me," Shevi admitted with her typical candor. "I don't enjoy acting. I'm embarrassed. I'm afraid. But I feel that…I have to help you. It's no great thing to do only what you like. I'll get over my stage fright for you. As long as you tell the director it's me, so it won't be a lie."

"You," Riki said as she hugged her twin tightly, "are the best sister in the world!!"

Shevi grinned. "Don't exaggerate. But I really *am* a good sister...."

They laughed. Riki's tears dried up and her eyes began to sparkle. They headed out of the room, hand in hand, to tell Ima and Abba about their decision.

## Chapter 36

# Shevi Saves the Show

With shaky legs, Shevi began to walk to the stage dressed in the Clara costume that Riki was supposed to be wearing!

But the secret was safe, so as not to ruin things for Riki. Shevi knew the part well but she was still scared. She walked out of the dressing room into the dim corridor leading to the stage. Her hands groped the walls as she went. How would she know if she was wearing the right hat? What if the heavy necklace she was wearing fell off?

Enough. Shevi pushed away her fears, and told herself in a whisper: *Hashem is with me. Everything will be fine.* She went over to the sound technician, who affixed a small mic to her collar.

Shevi walked onto the stage, squinting in the bright lights after being in that dark hallway. Her shaking hands were covered in gloves, and her voice was almost a whisper: "Is that you, Aunt Rivka?"

Shevi acted well. She surprised herself when she didn't make a single mistake; her performance was realistic, and even moved people to tears.

When the play was over, the curtain came down, and then back up again. The audience clapped, and Shevi, excited and blushing, hurried off the stage so she could escape....

"It was such *nachas* for me, to see my daughter put aside her own feelings and perform for her sister." Ima looked at Shevi lovingly. "Did you enjoy performing?"

"Yes, very much," Shevi admitted. "It was so amazing, that for a minute I forgot who I am, and that I'm not the actress, my sister is."

"What?!" Miri said. (She entered the room that minute.) "You were the actress, not Riki?"

"Not exactly." Shevi was as honest as ever. "Because everyone *thought* it was her! I was her understudy. I took her place for a day."

Night came, and the house settled down to sleep. In her mind, Shevi flashed back to the events of the day. She knew it was a day she'd never forget. The fear, the uncertainty, and the hard decision. Most of all: going onto the stage in a costume and surprising herself as she played the part of Clara very well. She hadn't expected that. Could it be that she really did know how to act? And liked it? Could it be that she had always known how to act but her stage fright had prevented her from doing it?

The cool night breeze chilled Shevi's flaming cheeks, and she suddenly felt someone come over to her and whisper, "Shevi?"

"Abba!" She turned around, smiling shyly at her father. "I couldn't fall asleep...."

"Of course, I understand. I heard all about it," Abba said. "You're probably too excited to sleep. Do you want to tell me how it all went?"

"But you know!" Shevi was confused.

"That's right, so what? I know what others told me. But I don't feel like I know how *you* felt. Tell me, Shevi, okay?"

"Sure!" As Shevi shared her feelings it helped her to calm down. Abba looked at his glowing daughter, and his heart swelled with pride. He smiled at her.

"So, are you happy, Abba?"

"Of course I'm happy that it went so well for you." Abba was taken aback at the question.

"No, I'm asking if you're happy that...I'm not—" Shevi felt very awkward, but she kept going: "That I'm not so quiet and shy?"

Abba's eyebrows shot up. "I love my daughter as she is," he declared. "If there is anything that I am not sure of, it's whether you love yourself the way you are."

"Why, because I'm quiet and shy?"

"Yes."

"I like to be quiet," Shevi said candidly. "I don't like noise and tumult. But I also don't like being so shy."

"So there you go," Abba said with a smile. "Hashem sent you this gift to help you shake off some of your shyness, and to stay the wonderful girl you are, just without as much shyness."

"Some people like to be shy."

"And that's fine, and nice. It's a good Jewish *middah*," Abba said. Then he whispered, "You know I was also shy once."

"Really?!" Shevi gasped. "You're not shy at all!"

"Life teaches you all kinds of things." He winked. "There's a time to be shy and a time to be outgoing."

The next day, the real performance took place. The twenty-five-year anniversary celebration went off without a hitch. The audience was far bigger than the day before. Riki, whose voice had thankfully recovered by then, took to the stage and performed beautifully. The Schneider girls gazed admiringly at their sister.

Most of the audience the day before did not know about the switch. In fact, Etty heard someone whispering to her friend, "Yesterday, she also performed like that! Exactly the same!"

The director, however, who did know about the switch, praised Shevi to her mother. "It's unbelievable that such a young girl, whom I didn't even train and who only read the script and practiced on her own, was able to perform so convincingly!" she exclaimed. "Why didn't she sign up for the play?"

"She didn't know," Ima explained. "She didn't know that she could act. She's just too shy."

"Maybe she would like to join my drama club?" the director suggested. Shevi, who was listening, blushed. Ima squeezed her hand encouragingly.

"Do you want to? Your school lets you join these clubs."

Shevi glowed. "Do you let?"

"Yes, sweetie." Ima smiled at her lovingly. "You see? When someone does *chessed* for others, Hashem makes sure there is good in it for him, too."

Chapter 37

# A Visit to the Dentist

"I would never have believed," Lali said, tying a yellow ribbon around Buma's horns, "that you would go up there and perform and then go sign up for a drama club."

"Me neither," Shevi agreed. She kept a safe distance from Buma, who bleated a satisfied "beh" every few minutes. Buma was busy, trying to lick whatever she could reach. "But after I performed, I realized that I really like acting, and maybe it will help me overcome my shyness. I'm so excited!"

"That's it," Lali said with a triumphant grin. "When your dream comes true you feel like you want to make others' dreams come true. It all started with my amazing dream that came true, and that was to raise an animal in the house."

234 Under 1 Roof

"Yoni's birds don't count?" Shevi hoped, deep down, that Lali would agree to become friends with the birds and would send Buma back to wherever she came from.

"Nah." Lali waved off the idea. "That's not enough. You can't compare a pigeon to a lamb!"

"I'm not comparing," Shevi murmured, a bit dejectedly. Her hopes had been dashed.

"At first, you didn't like those pigeons either, and then you got used to them," Lali reminded her.

"Well, I sort of got used to them," Shevi answered carefully. She was afraid that Lali would ask her to get used to Buma. Lali gently stroked her lamb, and Buma responded with a: "Beh!" She opened her mouth, and Lali peeked inside. She gasped. "Wait a minute!" she cried. "She doesn't have teeth! She has no top teeth! Not even one! She has no teeth at all!"

"What about teeth? Who said anything about teeth?" Shevi asked.

"Me!" Nechamy bounded into the girls' room with a wail. "I forgot! And our committee made up to meet to plan the class picnic today!"

"What?" Lali got up to put Buma back in her pen. Shevi stayed to listen to her sister.

"I have a dentist appointment today and I have no time to go!" In a weaker voice Nechamy added, "Or patience…I hate the dentist! The smell makes me nauseous and the noise gives me the chills…."

"So cancel the appointment," Shevi suggested calmly.

"I can't!" Nechamy was almost hysterical, which was not like her. "Because then we have to pay for the treatment. And if we cancel the appointment so close to the time then we have to pay for it anyway. What a waste of money!"

"So, is that your dream?" Lali came back to the room and heard the tail end of her sister's problem. Her eyes began to twinkle.

"Yes!" Nechamy grasped on to the idea. "You want to make everyone's dreams come true, right? Great, here's a dream: If you get the dentist's office to cancel my appointment — without us paying money — that would be an amazing dream come true."

"I'll try." Lali took the phone and left the room. She walked to the kitchen, where there was a list of important phone numbers on the fridge. Among them, she knew, was the phone number of the dentist's office.

~~~

"You can't cancel the appointment!" the secretary informed Lali. "If you cancel less than twenty-four hours before, then you have to pay a fee of one hundred and fifty shekels."

"And if I make an appointment for someone else instead?"

"That's fine. If someone comes in your place, then you don't have to pay the cancellation fee, because the appointment wasn't cancelled."

"Okay, so I want to make the appointment for someone else. Write Buma instead of Nechama," Lali stressed.

"Alright," the secretary said. "Whatever the name is. But come on time."

"*Im yirtzeh Hashem.*" Lali hung up with mixed feelings. On the one hand, she was happy: Someone would check why Buma had no top teeth. Maybe it was a problem? On the other hand...uh...something told her that the dentist would not be pleased at all....

"The appointment is cancelled!" she announced when she marched into Nechamy's room.

"You cancelled the appointment for me?" Nechamy's face lit up and she leaped out of her chair. "Thanks, Lali! That's a real dream come true...I can't stand the smell at the dentist's office!"

"Oh, come on," Ayala scoffed. "You're going to have to go a different time."

"I'll worry about it then," Nechamy smiled. "Meanwhile, I'm going to Elisheva's house today. Then we'll go to the meeting together. When Ima comes home please tell her that you were able to cancel the appointment without paying, and that I'll go a different time, of course."

"Fine." Lali was a bit nervous. Would the dentist be very unhappy about checking Buma? Can't be. She was a dentist, and what was the difference?! Out of caution, Lali decided to take one person with her. Who? Etty, of course. She was the only one whom Lali even considered taking along to such an appointment. She walked to Etty's room, and found her on her bed reading.

"You made an appointment for Buma?" Etty was astonished by Lali's request. "Did Ima let? How are you going to go on the bus? And why does she need a dentist?"

"Ima's not home, and I told Ayala that I'm going somewhere. She let me." Lali answered the questions in order. "About the bus, I'll walk. The dentist isn't far."

"Right." Etty stretched. "I remember when we went for checkups half a year ago."

"And why does she need a dentist? Because all her top teeth are missing! Poor thing, maybe she has a problem? Maybe she's sick? She needs a dentist to check her!"

"You're right."

"Are you coming?" Lali asked impatiently.

"Of course." Etty wouldn't miss an adventure like this. "What's the question? Let's go to the clinic!"

 **Chapter 38**

# Secret of the Missing Teeth

So the two girls and the little lamb left the house. Lali was first, leading Buma with a rope (Buma had been very polite in the elevator and hadn't bleated even once! That way, none of the neighbors knew that something else was using the elevator....) Etty followed along behind Buma, waving away a bunch of bothersome flies — and a noisy group of children who were curiously following the lamb.

The walk was more or less uneventful, except for the two or three children who escorted them to the clinic. There were no adults around to ask any questions. Lali knew the hardest part was still ahead, so she was a bit quiet, which was very unlike her. Etty was very excited about their latest adventure. She didn't know how happy the dentist would be to see Buma, but she was sure she'd at least check a cute little lamb that might be suffering from a disease. She was a dentist, right?! And dentists and doctors always need to help the sick!

They got to the door and knocked.

"Come in!" they heard a voice.

Lali pushed the door a bit. Then a bit more. She peeked inside carefully.

"Yes, yes, you can come in!" the secretary called. "Come on inside! Are you here yourself?! Good for you, brave girl. Even some of the adults come with another person. But dear, I'm not sure that we are allowed to treat you if there's no adult with you. By law—"

"You're not allowed to?" Lali's face fell. "Till I got here…. Why isn't it allowed?"

"Because you're a minor. Are you Buma Schneider?"

"No, that's not me and I'm not alone." Lali tugged gently at the rope, and Buma stepped importantly into the clinic. "Here is Buma. Is she a minor?"

The secretary gasped and looked very confused. She froze and then leaped up and jumped onto her chair. "What is this cow doing here?!"

"It's not a cow," Etty protested, as she stepped inside and closed the door politely. "She's a lamb. A little lamb."

"Little?!" the secretary squeaked. "She's huge!"

"No she's not, she's not even a year old!"

"And what is she doing here?"

"She needs a dentist," Lali insisted. "She has no top teeth!"

"Help!" the secretary screeched. "Dr. Michal!! Michal!! Michal Benziman!!! Dr. Michal!!"

"What's wrong?" The dentist opened her door and peeked into the waiting room. "What—" She stopped in shock. "What is this?! Who is this?! Who are you?"

"This is Buma Schneider," Lali said quietly. "And I'm Lali. This is my sister Etty, and this is my lamb."

"Why did you come here?" The doctor, in contrast to the secretary who had scrambled onto her chair in sheer fright, was calm. She didn't look surprised or frightened.

"I came so you can check her."

"I'm not a veterinarian," the dentist said calmly, as if she was talking to a little girl who had come for a checkup. "You need to take her to an animal doctor."

"Oh," Lali said disappointed. "but I don't know any...I thought, you're a dentist, and she has a problem with her teeth—"

"I'm a dentist for human teeth."There was a mischievous glint in the dentist's eye. "In any case, what is— what did you call her?"

"Buma."

"So what is Buma's problem?"

"She has no top teeth."

"Get her out of here!!!" the secretary screeched hysterically. She could not believe that the dentist was actually talking to this girl and her lamb. "Fast!"

"No need, everything is fine." A smile played on the dentist's lips. "I grew up on a moshav. I'm not afraid of sheep or goats...I grew up with them! But do you know why she doesn't have top teeth?"

"Maybe because she's still small and they are going to grow?" Lali sensed that she had found a listening ear.

"No." The dentist's smile widened. "It's because all kosher animals do not have top teeth. So you can cancel her appointment."

"Do I have to pay a hundred and fifty shekels?" Lali gasped.

"No," the dentist laughed. "It's on me. A gift for Buma."

"Oh, thank you," Lali gushed. "So everything is okay?"

"Yes."

"Good, so I'll make a new appointment for my sister," Lali said to the sectary, who had carefully gotten off the desk back onto the swivel chair.

"First, get the lamb out of here!"

"But what about Nechamy's appointment?"

"Is Nechamy also a sheep?" the secretary's voice shook. "A lamb?"

"No, of course not!" Lali answered innocently. "How could that be? She's my sister! If she was a lamb, then I'd also have to be a lamb, right? And I'm not, so it's not possible!"

"I don't know," the secretary muttered shakily, "what is possible and what is not. It's not possible that a lamb came to our clinic instead of a girl…."

On the way home, Lali was cheerful. *"Baruch Hashem*, everything is fine with Buma." She put her hand dramatically on her heart. "Now my heart feels much lighter."

"Yes," Etty agreed, "and you also finished making Nechamy's dream come true."

"Oh," Lali sighed, sounding like an adult. "That's right. But I still have a lot of work left to do."

"What kind of work?"

"I'm only partway through the family. I have to make another fourteen Schneider dreams come true!"